RAIDERS OF THE
LOW-FOREHEAD

by
STANLEY MANLY

ATTACK! is an imprint of Creation Books.

First published in 1999 by ATTACK! Books
83 Clerkenwell Road, London EC1 5AR
Copyright: Stanley Manly 1999
Design by Rom
Original artwork by Paul McAffery
Printed and bound in Great Britain by
Woolnough Book Binding Ltd
Irthlingborough, North Hants

RAIDERS OF THE LOW FOREHEAD is a a work of avant-pulp
fiction. Any similarities between characters in this book and real
people, alive or dead, is entirely coincidental.

WARNING! Reading ATTACK! books in an enclosed space can
result in violent epileptic fits involving much thrashing, writhing and
foaming at the mouth and - in extreme cases - attempts to chew
off one's own face. If in any doubt, please consult a doctor before
continuing.

ABOUT THE AUTHOR

STANLEY MANLY WROTE THIS BOOK.

01 - SEX

She was hot.
He was randy.
She was easy.
His meat was hard.
He met her on the quay-side when she knocked-off work.
She gutted fish like a real un'.
'Come on,' she said, 'let's do it.'
They did.

Then they went for chips.

02 - FOOD

The chip shop was hot. People were sweating in the chip shop the way they sweat in a chip shop when it is hot.

'It's hot in here.' he said.

'Yeah', she dripped, "I'm sweating.".

'CHIPS!' he demanded heroically, ramming a fiver into the counter and head-butting a pensioner in the ankles.

'Salt and vinegar?' asked the lass, hardly frugging at the twisted mass of Zimmer and teeth.

'YEAH!!!!!' roared the shop.

'That's somebody's old lad and you've done him in a pathetic attempt to impress a bird.' whispered a whinging wanker by the window. 'Anyway, everyone knows you're softer than shite.'

'There's doin' and there's doin'.' he argued reasonably. 'Me and my lass are dying for our chips.'

'YEAHHH!!!!!' roared the shop.

He grabbed the bag. Then he took the chips off the counter. As they hit the street, the shop was hitting the wanker in the window.

They sat on a dead dog and he made to open the bag a bit.
'I fucked you and fed you.' he said romantically.
'What's yer name?'

'SHARON, SHARON GOER.' she stated. 'What's yours?'

'VINCE,' he vectored, 'VINCE EAGER.'

'You can say that again.' she sounded.

'VINCE,' he vectored, 'VINCE EAGER.'

'So you're EAGER and I'm a bit of a GOER, that should
work out. Do you think we could make it happen?' she gobbled.

'Not yet,' he body-swerved, sweating over his reserves of seed,
'I'm still eating me chips.'

'Don't you want me to eat you with my gob all hot from chips
and that?'

His buttocks stiffened and his manhood clenched. Nearby a
UFO hovered over the docks and sent green-eyed squid messengers to
ask earthlings where that Vera Lynn, sweetheart of the forces in World
War II, lived.
'She's grown up with kids now.' blurted a passing bloodhound
telepathically. 'Don't you bastards understand anything about
relativity?'
'Relatively little,' slobbered a squid, gutted.
'Anyway' the dog went on, 'I'd give this planet a wide one. I
wouldn't treat a dog the way these human bastards treat us.'

Just then his buttocks stiffened and his manhood clenched.
'........with my gob all hot from chips and that?' she said.

'Yeah,' he grunted like a bloke, 'just heat up your gob with
the whole packet. Good chips eh?'

They were. Thick slices of fresh potato fried in the best quality fat. Each chip erupted into a succulent warm mush, coating their tongues with lingering waves of glowing and substantial satisfaction. The salt stuck to their lips and the vinegar cut into the sides of their mouths - exploding them into caverns of bursting, pulsating, teasing and tasteful light.

But VINCE's jumbo sausage was crap.

'Decent bag of chips this.' she slobbered poetically.

'Get off our dog.' rasped a voice dryer than a Saudi slag's gash.

Vince put down his bag. Then he handed her the last of his chips.

'You'll die before you speak about my slag like that.' he threatened, noisily.

'No we haven't.' stated a bloke, obviously.

In a lightning burst of fury he ripped into the bloke like lightning. Seconds later, he bounced off like a seven stone weakling and apprentice sex-god with no hard qualities worth shit to his name.

'Something just struck me.' rasped the slow-witted sort with the Saudi slag sound. 'We wasn't talking 'bout yer bit of slack, son. We wuz just sayin' thanks fer keepin' us dog warm.'

'I can keep myself warm, thanks.' said SHARON in a rare out-burst of militant feminism.

'Not you, bitch. We wuz on about the dog, the thing you're sitting on' said the gash gob and his mob.

Later, VINCE said ..... 'So you three people including the geezer with the gob that sounds like a Saudi slag's gash are tramps and this dead dog on the ground near where me and my bird are sitting is your dinner. And in addition to that you three decided to get some mustard

8

to give your flea ridden meal an up-market feel and for this you left the dog and stood beside a burger van threatening to drop your trousers if the man didn't make with the mustard?'

'Well summarised, so,.' gurgled gash-gob.

'Well fuck me if it isn't a UFO full of green-eyed squid taking off from the docks,' talked a tramp.

'Yer a dozy bastard if yer think I'm gonna fall for that one again.' said another. 'I'm turnin' me back on this slice of dog for nowt.'

'Come with me,' cooed SHARON.

He did.

Passing the chip shop he said 'Frig.'

'Finger first,' she drooled, hardly frugging.

A mob looked up from walloping a whinging wanker in the window.

'YEAH!!!!!!!!' roared the shop.

Later, a pensioner picked himself up off the chip shop floor, gathered the false teeth he'd thrown around him and re-arranged his collapsable Zimmer frame.
'That out-for-the-count crap fools 'em every time,' he thought to himself.
'But most of the sadistic young tykes that try to roll me hit harder than that pathetic sod with that fit looking lass in tow.'
He shuffled away, feeling in his pocket the rolled up twenty quid in used fivers he had taken from VINCE to stage the dive and help VINCE look hard in front of his new bird.

03 - VIOLENCE

In the chip shop, fists flew furiously in a furious fistful fracas.

STIG BIG, ELVIS TWAT and TYRONE HOODLUM arrived. They'd been clocking the action from a distance and now they decided to cut the distance, stop clocking and get into the action.

'We're THE RAIDERS OF THE LOW FOREHEAD and you lot are dead.' they announced, reasonably. Everyone in the chip shop was still alive, but they got the general idea.

Soon, STIG BIG, ELVIS TWAT and TYRONE HOODLUM were wasting a wanker wonderfully. STIG BIG screamed: 'You've had yer chips now, WANKER!' Ripping the life out of total strangers with his bare hands brought out the thoughtful side of STIG.

'Well actually I haven't had them yet. You see I ordered chicken and that takes ten minutes and then that EAGER chappie with the young girl pushed in, so that held things up a little bit and when he head butted that pensioner in the ankles, well to be frank ...'

'WANKER!' howled TYRONE HOODLUM.

RIP !
WHAM !
SPLAT !
'MUMMY !'

Fists flew furiously in a furious fistful fracas. Ripping into a face with his teeth, STIG BIG spat slices and filled his gob with gore.

Kicking the wanker in the head with all he had, TYRONE HOODLUM found some more to rip out his heart and make it personally responsible for the years of unspeakable torment he had suffered at the hands of his father, SIR CLEMENT HOODLUM.

'YOU WAIT TILL YOUR FATHER GETS HOME !' he howled at the heart. 'YOU'RE IN FOR A SEVERE CHASTISEMENT, YOUNG MAN.'

The heart ignored him and just bled.

Outside a UFO full of green-eyed squid skidded to a halt.
'It's fast and furious' agreed the Captain, 'but the obvious lack of noisy weaponry suggests that World War II is indeed over.'
The UFO full of green-eyed squid skidded to a take off.

Fists flew furiously in furious fistful fracas. Fat fists put fat lips on fat faces.

'RUCK, SARGE!' roared a rozzer running.

'PIGS!' blagged ELVIS TWAT, twatting a prat and making him splat.

'That'll be £8.29 with both o' them pickled eggs,' said the lass, hardly figging at the seething mass of splintering faces. A punter paid for his chips and split.

'There's some BIG TWATTING HOODLUMS in there,' rasped a rozzer, clocking STIG BIG, ELVIS TWAT and TYRONE HOODLUM.

'It's them three again. You know, ELVIS, STIG and TYRONE. The RAIDERS OF THE LOW FOREHEAD. Could be dodgy, Sarge.'

Hardly wigging, the Sarge walked in.

'Are you lot gonna come down the station or do we have to come in and getcha?' said the Sarge.

'YEAH!' roared the shop. 'OFFICIAL!'

04 - SEX

Later, when VINCE got her home, he ripped out a couple of lagers and hit her with some R KELLY. They frugged, frigged, fumbled and fingered. Then they wellied, wobbled and watched a video. 'FUCK ME !' she fraggled in her best Pauline Quirk. 'Do I love me foreplay or WHAT!!!!?'

Then they had sex.

'DESSERT?' drooled VINCE, over the fanny farts, pulling out.

'TOO RIGHT !' she roared , making like a bucket. 'Let's have some sloppy seconds!'

'Later!' he wigged, seedless and stalling for time. Flipping R KELLY for NOELANDLIAM, he did a LINFORD for the kitchen and tore chunks from a YORKIE. Culling a carton of custard from the cupboard, he chunked up the top with the YORKIE and threw in his last half of CARAMAC.

She moaned as she munched on a chunk and smeared herself on the carpet. 'If there's one thing that gets me wetty, sweaty, horny and hot it's the satisfying chunk that only YORKIE has got.'

Licking the custard from a lump, VINCE bit hard on the brick and felt the stupendous, solid, creamy magnificence slowly spread over his tongue. Careering through the shag pile in orgasmic rapture, he allowed his tongue to caress the deepest corners of his mouth, seeking out the secret, sweet, staccato delights of the slowly fading fragments.

Each sweet burst came with lingering after-shocks that slowed his breathing, stretching seconds into hours as he fought to hang on to the dying delights of the YORKIE.

By comparison, the Caramac was crap.

Later she said:

'My Dad and little brother are in jail for a crime they didn't commit and I'd swallow it for life from anybody who'd get the bastards who did it and bring about a tearful reunion for the torn and ragged tribe of rejects that is the terrible remnant of my family. It was STIG BIG, ELVIS TWAT and TYRONE HOODLUM that did for my Dad and our lad. They don't even know who I am but I saw them lurking as we were leaving the chippie tonight and it reminded me, like how people in a movie sometimes see an important character at the start and it reminds them of stuff that ends up making the story happen.'

06 - VIOLENCE

'Them bastards ate one of my men,' roared the Sarge, tearful and almost sensitive.

'OFFICIAL!' growled STIG BIG spitting a helmet.

Bodies, blood and bucketed wanker paddled from a paddy wagon and poured themselves into the police station. The copper on the desk eyed the mob like how a copper on a desk eyes a mob in a TV show about coppers, mobs and desks.

'Eye eye,' said an inspector, inspecting. 'What's the score ?'

'Psycho 1 Plod 0' said STIG BIG, ELVIS TWAT and TYRONE HOODLUM together, finding strength and comradeship in the best boy scout tradition.

Shit, spat the copper on the desk.
'You dirty bastard' growled the Sarge. 'I hope you floss before you snog your missus.'

Men growled, then they growled some more. By the time they'd growled again they were really growling. There was one dead copper, three smug psychos and hell to pay. If they'd had brains their looks would have been meaningful. They didn't, so they just gave each other looks. Then the fight started.

It started with a 'BASTARDS!'

Police boots, big sticks and a length of lead pipe went in. ELVIS TWAT bit lumps and spat them out. The ruck rumbled round the room. STIG BIG was the first to break cover.

'That bastards broken the cover, Sarge' complained a copper.

'Your life's in danger and you wade in with a shit joke about breaking cover. Fucking pathetic' called the Sarge. Then he added, 'I'm going in, cover me. Ooh, it's the way I tell 'em.'

The Sarge barged as cops chopped and the speeding STIG was grabbed by the pigs. 'DUMB-SHIT, MEATHEAD, MOTHERFUCK, BASTARDS!' he said, reasonably. 'It strikes me that you chaps are using an unnecessary degree of force in this act of restraint upon my person.'

'It's necessary .... to kill yer!' spat the Sarge. He got to do all the best talking bits.

Just then STIG BIG, ELVIS TWAT and TYRONE HOODLUM got mad. TYRONE HOODLUM disarmed a copper. He did it by ripping his arms off. Crimson gore stained the floor as TYRONE crushed the law man's paw. Crawling from the mass of seething constabulary, ELVIS TWAT ripped out a concealed weapon and hid it in a head. STIG BIG punched, butted, wrenched and gutted his way to the top of the mob. Then he ripped the giblets from a raw recruit.

'GUTTED!' he yelled in triumph.

Later, STIG BIG, ELVIS TWAT and TYRONE HOODLUM said:
'Killin' coppers is serious crime and we might go down for a long long time. We never left no witnesses in the police station but it would be smart to fit somebody for the crime like how we fitted that geezer and his son before.'

07 - SEX

In the cold light of morning she was FIT. The firm contours of her breasts tapering to reddened bullets. The firm muscles of her arms rippling to gut fish.

'Come on,' VINCE mumbled into the pillow, grasping hopefully on a haunch.

'They'll be waiting down the factory.' she protested, sensibly. 'There's seventeen tons of mackerel to be ripped apart with my bare hands.'

Going for it, he took a deep breath and said: 'I'm growing a lump and I'm up for a pump!'

'Oh you sweet talker, I never could resist it.'

RIP !
SQUEAK, SQUEAK, SQUEAK.

'Yes, yes, yEs, YE-YE-YES, YE-E-E-E-S, OOHHHHH YEEESSSSSS!'

PUMMEL PUMMEL PUMMEL
Heurchh, nn, ugh, ugh
'Yes, yes......ahhhhhh.........YES!!!!!!!!
[squelch, squelch, squelch]

'UGH!'

'See ya.'

08 - FOOD

STIG BIG , ELVIS TWAT and TYRONE HOODLUM were heading home. They'd had a fight. They'd had ten fights. Each. It had been a good night but now it was a bad morning cos they were HUNGRY.

Innocently, a burger van came into sight.

Viciously, they stopped it.

'GIZ IT,' grunted TYRONE HOODLUM who had a way with words.

'Have you got any money?'

'HAVE YOU GOT A FAMILY?'

MUNCH, MUNCH, MUNCH.

The pungent pot pourrie of peeled potatoes, prime pulped beef, low-priced pork and pizza slices poured into the ravenous threesome making them all gleesome. Their slobbering gobs got on with the job.

STIG BIG feasted on pig, his monstrous tongue chased a chunk into his throat, left at the epiglottis and back with a cough and a vengeance to impact on the inside of his front teeth. The sliver of sausage split apart, leaving its fatty contents within reach of tortured taste buds. The cheap spices and cheerless fat revived a mouth that felt all flat. The chewy lightness brought a brightness. STIG savoured the fleeting firmness of the flavour that clung to his lips. He marvelled at the sharp peppery primary tang followed by the slight but solid fatty linger of the easily under-rated long pork finger. Chewing a chunk to a soft pulp he rolled it around, smearing sausage all round his mouth.

A week before, in a factory two dozen miles away, a bored and surly teenage girl had thought about a boyfriend who belched and bonked at the same time. His spotty bum and sweaty palms sent her into retching retreat. Then again, he could, when she played with his mind some, put in the effort to make her come. At the weekend she'd go looking for something better but in the meantime she would face the thrashing vat of pork sausage mix and add pepper. In fact, as she'd been dreaming about a better class of squirt getting his hands up her skirt, she'd already gone well over the pepper limit for this batch. Oh well, cheap pepper or not, these hot dogs would bite back a little.

Now the budget seasoning awakened STIG'S reasoning. Ripping into the rocks of bread littered around the van, STIG noticed his mood moderating, his chest starting to heave and shameless sheep images shuffling through his slowly grinding grey matter. Tonight, fortified with cheap meat and that happy glow that only head breaking can provide, he would make his move.

09 - VIOLENCE

There was a crowd.
It was raining.
A bus was coming.
It was full, nearly.

The crowd were off to collect their pension.
They had little cash and lots of tension.
In the crowd were blokes and biddies.
In their pants were lines of skiddies.

'How's yer gusset Gertie?' butted an elderly bloke at a piece of skirt he'd once tried to poke.

'Steamin' and streamin'' she batted back with feeling.

'How come?'

'You've got me,' admitted Gertie, 'I can't figure it out but every-time I imagine myself getting old and incontinent I just shit myself with fear.'

'That's a tough one,' admitted the bloke.

'Nah, it's squashy and seeping' she oozed back.

The bus stopped. 'Room for three up top,' said the conductor, hopefully.

It was hopeless.

People ran.
The conductor didn't.
He stood up.
Then he fell down.

The blokes in the throng couldn't go wrong. They'd seen it all at Dunkirk so storming buses was easy work.

Handbag wielding grannies fought to the death over a square foot of leather, and we ain't talking about their skins here.

Feeble bloke memories recalled stormed beaches. The women didn't stand a chance. During the days of the Dunkirk spirit, they'd been at home knobbing balaclavas and knitting yanks.

Zimmers flailed and fists flew, the bus was abandoned by its crew.

The kind of reasonable tosser that always stands on the sidelines and talks toss said: 'They really should lay on extra buses when they know there are a lot of people going into town on a Thursday to collect their pension.'

WHUMP !

That man had tossed his last.

Coming upon the seething mass with gobfulls of burger, STIG BIG, ELVIS TWAT and TYRONE HOODLUM wiped off their juices and made with a plan.

B-S-E'd to breaking point, STIG BIG broke. He broke arms, legs, heads, pelvises and a seat. The bus was silent, except for the sounds of STIG BIG, ELVIS TWAT and TYRONE HOODLUM coming on the scene.

Later TYRONE HOODLUM pulled into the police station and dumped his load.

ELVIS TWAT and STIG BIG kicked the comatose crowd into the cold crowd of coppers they'd callously clobbered the night before. Then TYRONE HOODLUM threw in a note. It said: "Us pensioners are gonna do the police. They have been harassing us and denying us our own parliament for too long. It may be a suicide mission but death is better than living death."

FRAMED!!!!

10 - SEX

VINCE's aunt Dorothy knew a bit about STIG BIG, ELVIS TWAT and TYRONE HOODLUM. She knew a bit about everybody cos she used to work for the police. He went round thinking blow jobs for life. She answered the door thinking nose jobs now.

She sat on his face.

He couldn't hear the stereo.

'MOVE, YOU BITCH!' he screamed into the wobbling flesh. In thirty seconds flat he'd learned to breathe through his skin. Within a minute he was having an out-of-body experience. Ten seconds after that the convulsions started.

'OOOOH!!!' she sighed, 'Ooooh, oooh, OOOOOOHHHH AAAAAAAHHHHHHH !!!!!!!!!!!!!!!!!!!!!'

His nose hit clit and did it's bit. He weathered the deluge of batter and sucked down seventeen pints of air when she spilled onto the floor.

His soul stopped somewhere above the hot water tank, turned round and floated back into his body.

'Now then Lovey, I'll make the tea,' she smiled slapping on her stupendous drawers and wobbling into the kitchen. 'Lucky for you your Uncle Percy is still in hospital.'

'Yeah,' grunted VINCE. 'Tell me, what did bring on his heart attack?'

Later, his aunt Dorothy said: "Them lads you mentioned are well known to the police. STIG BIG, ELVIS TWAT and TYRONE HOODLUM are hard bastards. They've got muscles like steel, no morals worth speaking of and a tendency to erupt into action at the slightest provocation.'

'Yeah,' he grunted. 'Anything else?'

'Ooh, I wish them lads was round 'ere now!' she dribbled.

Retching unnaturally VINCE, started to split. 'Thanks, Aunty Dorothy,' he grunted. 'I'll remember that.'

11 - FOOD

VINCE needed to think. TYRONE HOODLUM, STIG BIG and ELVIS TWAT needed to think, but they couldn't.

VINCE thought, then he thought some more. By the time he'd thought again he decided he needed time to think. He thought all the thinking was doing his brain in.

He had to eat.

His Aunt Dorothy's deluge of batter had battered his bonce to breaking point. There was a cafe, he made a break for it.

'Fried, fried, fried or fried dear?' said the big lass turning on the gas.

'Over easy,' he grunted as the rashers hit the pan.
'What, me or the bacon?'

She looked like two pigs fighting in an apron but VINCE had never met a pig with B.O. that bad. He was gonna heave. 'Shut the fuck up and just bloody cook it.' he put in tactfully.

The plate arrived without another word.

Gently dribbling grease onto the white china, the bacon was a sight to behold. Two glistening eggs made up the sides of the plate and sausages thicker than a man's pricker spanned them like how a bridge spans a river.

The bacon oozed tasty fat onto his tongue and the sausage lay there promising a firm follow up. Each sample of the prime back slice was a sensation of serious dimensions. His battered brain came back again.

The sausage was seductive but he went for the eggs next. One yolk exploded on his tongue and slopped into the ditches outside his teeth. The strength and consistency of the four grain free range wonder coupled with the low-cost lard to make the taste hard. VINCE could feel the last drips of egg falling from the sides of his mouth and landing in the pools at the bottom. He let the eggs take their time. The slippery white bits slid around his mouth, coating everything. He saved the crispy bit where it had last touched the pan to the very end.

VINCE stuck it between his front teeth and ran his tongue behind them, breaking bits off and feeling the crackles. He could taste the fat that had soaked into this bit of the egg and in that fat there was a hint of SAUSAGE !!!!!!!

He just had to have that porky bastard, NOW! His knife slashed a slice off the end. The skin was shining with a brown colour underneath. Inside it was as pink as what his baby brother used to look like. It was steaming and dripping. He could smell a hint of pepper but mostly this baby was solid meat.

Outside it was the same old grey cesspit of a town. In his gob it was Nagasaki. The flavour hit 200 on the Richter scale and he grabbed the table to steady himself. The meaty magnificence of the prime pork was fighting its way to every taste bud. When it got there it beat the shit out of egg dregs and proceeded to assault his senses. Within half a sausage he could feel the pepper burning into the skin on the roof of his mouth and sending pulses of pleasure every few seconds. His gob was all a throb as the porker did its job.

After a full sausage his mouth was alive with heat and flavour. The peppery edge and succulent steam fought their way up his nose and extra taste sensation just about blew the top of his head off. VINCE swallowed the squashy slabs, slowly. Savouring every split second of slithering and thanking fuck that they were dithering as they coated his throat with flavour.

By the time he was down to his last forkful of the porkful prize banger his brain was back and he'd made an important decision.

'Hey,' he bellowed at the big lass, 'I'll have another plateful of this lot.'

12 - VIOLENCE

Things were seriously serious in the police station. Dead coppers, stunned pensioners, twisted metal. And the coffee machine hadn't worked since STIG BIG broke the cover.

'I've put in over a pound,' said an old granny, 'and all I get is hot water.'

'Have you tried your bus tokens?' asked another one, slowly coming round and missing the mass of Zimmer frames and bodies.

'Yes,' said the old lass, 'but my tokens just turn the water black and they taste terrible.'

The one on the floor clocked the death and destruction all around.

'Bugger me backwards with a badger's bum brush, what the fuck happened here?' she said daintily. Through a haze she half recalled a bus and a fight. Blurry shapes butted and gutted their way through her mind but the less blurry her mind became the more she realised that the shapes, the fight and the death and destruction that presented itself dripping off the walls and landing at her feet were just so much horrible reality. She was surrounded by twisted Zimmers and totalled bodies, plagued by thoughts of bus stop carnage and grimly aware that the slopping sound she could hear was provided by the sickly red gloop that was leaking from the gaping neck wound of some creature in a police uniform which hung, impaled and clearly dead, on a coat hook.

The pensioner on the floor realised that nothing in eighty one years of life, forty seven years of marriage and at least three desperate battles to fend off her late husband's insatiable interest in anal sex had prepared her for this moment in her life. Desperately she summoned her reserves of experience to find the words that would do justice to the scene. 'Bugger me backwards with a badger's bum brush' she gasped, 'what the fuck happened here?'

'There is no need for such language,' said the dotty specimen still straining for a cuppa.

'Bloody hell' said the bewildered bag on the floor. 'Our friends and all these coppers look like they're dead.'

'All in good time, dear' said the one at the machine. 'I'm sure things will sort themselves out after a nice cup of tea.'

'You daft bag,' said the one on the floor, 'can't you see what's happened?'

'Can't you mind your manners?' said the doddery dingbat at the drinks dispenser.

'ARGHHHH!!!!' screamed the one on the floor in general despair.

The screaming sent the senile one psychotic. The one on the floor wasn't to know it but the brain-dead biddy buying the tea was crazed by chemicals collected from countless vending machines. She was also stupendously psychotic in the face of swearing. Damn close to total dementia, she was suffering vending machine chemical withdrawal of the worst kind.

Withdrawing from the machine the gormless granny withdrew a knitting needle from her handbag and set out to withdraw the eyeballs from the other one.

Slashing through the air the needle hit bone somewhere in the floored one's cheek. 'ARGHHH Fuck !!!!' screamed the floored one.

'You and your cheek,' slobbered the senile specimen sticking the other one again. She was out to lunch completely now. 'TAXI RANK, SHAG A YANK, HOME FOR TEA WITH HIS MONEY IN THE BANK' she screamed.

The other one had her marbles but no fight. She flailed, then she flailed some more. The next time she flailed she stuck her jugular vein on the needle and sprayed blood over six feet.

'Look at the mess you've made of those six feet,' accused the Alzhiemer's atrocity with the needle and no tea. 'You've covered their best shoes in congealing goo. That ain't exactly friendly. If I wasn't such a calm and collected person, your thoughtless spurting could reduce me to mild swearing.'

In general frustration the other one let out a final scream.

'ARGHHHHHHH !!!!!!!'

It was enough to attract the attention of the first copper on the new shift arriving at the station. Clocking the carnage and the spouting blood, he spouted.

'Shit, bastard, fuckin' hell,' he said, remembering the day on "Manliness In The Face Of A Crisis" from his police training.

The berserk biddy fingered a knitting needle. 'Please,' she said, 'mind your manners.'

13 - SEX

After a hard night of breaking heads and stuffing in cheap sausage, STIG BIG was having sex.

Magnificently, he mounted her.
Ruggedly, he rode her.
Shamelessly, he shagged her.
Firmly, he forced himself upon her.

Thrusting with manly thrusts, he gazed upon her spreadeagled form. He felt his heart and manhood swell together.

'I've waited for this moment for I doesn't know 'ow long' he cooed into her ear, yokel fashion. 'Now my pretty darlin', you be mine.'

His tree trunk arms rooted to the wooden headboard as the rhythm of their love began to build. The shadeless forty watt bulb lent an atmosphere. Sensing it, she dilated, a little.

'That be it, my darling,' he grunted, 'Let I in.'

His manhood was fit to burst and his heart was even fitter 'cos of how he had waited for this moment for so long and that.

His ruddy face ruddied and his strapping arms strapped as his racing blood raced.

'I be comin'! I be comin'!' he howled. His monstrous voice filled the hovel and sent three acres of yellowing wall paper crashing to the floor.

'OOOOOHHHHHHH ARRRRRRRR, my pretty darlin'!"
He shot his load with basic ruggedness and a tightening of his bum crack.

Crashing to the mattress he took an almighty breath.
'Oh tell I it were good for you, tell I, tell I!' he pleaded.

Fixing him with her deep brown eyes she slid from the bed and planted all four feet firmly on the floor.
'BAAA,' she bleated, ignoring him and making straight for the fresh turnip he'd used to lure her into the den. Her suspender belt snapped and hit him in the eye.

'Fuckin' Herdwicks!' he spat. 'They doesn't know the meanin' of gratitude.'

14 - FOOD

ELVIS TWAT dragged himself up the stairs and attacked the door. The burger was wearing off and he wanted more food. NOW !!!!!

'Oi, Mum, you second-hand slimy slag' he said cheerfully. 'We got any food or what?'

'Jam's ready on the bread,' she cackled back hardly wigging.

ELVIS TWAT roared into it. Three slices later he roared again.

'This fucking jam is well off!' he rumbled reasonably.

'Fooled ya!' said the second-hand slimy slag. 'I ran out of Claire Raynor's before I finished me bleed. That first slice had some of your stepfather's spunk in it cos he gave me a right good seeing to. How's it feel to chomp on yer old lasses' pant liners, you low life scum?' The cackle crunched up to cement mixer cacophony.

ELVIS TWAT fought the wretch that was rooting in his guts. Holding down the bread, blob and sperm he made for the stairs with an about- turn.

Clocking a burger van through the window he paddled onto the pavement, ripped off a tyre with his bare hands, grabbed a pen off the van man and wrote.

"GIVE US A FUCKIN' BURGER NOW OR ELSE I'LL THROW UP SO BAD YOU'LL SELL NOWT ELSE TODAY

Love ELVIS"

'You don't get me with that one, laddy' said the Van Man, ludicrously.

'HUERRRKKKKKKKKK, UGH UGH'

'OH FUCK, look what you've done to me counter, you mental bastard!'

'HUERKKKKKKK !!!!!
                    Urghhhh, urghhhh - [massive gulp of air] - URGH-
HHHH!!!!!!!!!!!, huallpp!'

Spewing up always gave ELVIS TWAT an appetite. He made for the gherkins, crunching on a corker with the consistency of a porker. He found that peculiarly clean taste of prime pickle assaulting his senses, leading him on to greater heights of ambition and eloquence than yer average TWAT!!

'Decent bit of pickle this, after a few of these a fella could string a sentence together' he thought. Viciously vinegaring a brace of french fries in a roll, ELVIS went for the simple satisfaction of stuffed stomach and spreading warmth. Gripped by gherkin, primed with pickled onions and tripping on a packet of Tortilla chips, ELVIS TWAT buttered bread and buttied himself into stupor.

True, the light floweriness of the pathetic roll crust and the tepid consistency of the gutless white insides defined new lows of cynical mass production in the British baking industry. But the baking fat cats, gormless prats and remote accountants in bowler hats, hadn't reckoned on ELVIS TWAT.

Mashing a layer of french fried apologies into the centre of a bun, he banged in burger relish, ground up gherkins and trimmed the lot with Tabasco sauce. His teeth slowly bit the bun, forcing out the

rench fries into a warm mush that prepared his mouth for the explosive
delights to follow. Wolfing the warmth he felt satisfaction spread from
his feet to his parting whilst in his mouth the fireworks were starting.
The ground gherkins were hard to tell from the flaccid french fried
mush until they hit the sides of his gob and danced spicy circles around
the inside of his cheeks. Here a hint of vegetable goodness, there a
sharp shock of pickled pleasure. Slowly, magnificently - with all the
assurance, authority and all round amazing athleticism of an ABA
boxing champion - the mighty, meatless munch delivered it's killer
punch.

The Tabasco explosion started on ELVIS's tongue and
travelled the length and breadth of his known universe in a split second.
Then again, allowing for the size of ELVIS's known universe, that isn't
saying a lot. The fearsome, firework sauce backed the snack with
mighty force.

It pushed the gherkins and fries to bursting point, flaming up
their flavour to the point of total savour. The Tabasco hit ELVIS's
throat like a cruise missile and steered itself with pin-point accuracy to
his guts wherein it proceeded to remind the assorted bread, gherkins
and french fried mulch that they were food and they'd better fucking
well act the part and leave ELVIS with a sense of satisfaction as a
reward for his psychopathic burger van assaulting. The stomach
contents got the message and ELVIS got a warm glow. Sorted.

In the circumstances his improvisation on the theme of
hopeless bread, predictable gherkins and low grade fat soaked potatoes
was a triumph of cack-brained ingenuity over a centuries-long cynical
slide into mass production blandness in the food industry. In similar
circumstances the lowly and oppressed peoples of the world have
celebrated such victories over their un-caring masters by gathering
around camp fires, fingering sexy Soviet-made assault rifles, puffing
earnestly on cigarettes and pondering ever more ambitious victories.
From such nuggets the downtrodden have plotted campaigns for
freedom that have sent the corrupt into lonely exile and offered
'windswept and interesting' status - with it's attendant benefit of a leg-
over for life - to many men with terrible teeth and blatant bad breath.

Dimly, in the back of his brain, ELVIS TWAT sensed the seriousness of his achievement. He considered its meaning and forced his beleaguered bonce into a plan that would honour his exploits. He thought, and he thought and he thought until he thought he was starting to get a headache. Then he decided..........to make another burger just like the last one.

Later, the burger van man sold nowt all day.

15 - VIOLENCE

The copper was confused. Then again, he was confused tying his shoelaces. He'd suggested three times that they put Velcro on police boots. If only he could have spelled "Velcro" then the history of the constabulary would have been changed. As it was everyone in the force knew him as the dozy git who filled the suggestion box with postcards covered in crayon drawings of blokes with big boots and happy smiles. If the lot upstairs who made decisions had sussed the revolutionary lack of laces in the pictures, things might have been different. As it was they got more work than the average lot of management in emptying the suggestion box plus a fairly undemanding set of snap cards for those long afternoons when they couldn't be arsed making decisions.

The crayon-crazy copper copped the situation. There was one biddy giving him grief. Another giving him spurts of blood in the eye. And a pile of carnage on the floor. Somewhere under the moaning mass of metal and geriatrics were bits of police tunic and some sarge's stripes.

The copper tried his best to describe the sight into his radio. 'Er .... Fuck !' he said.

'Come in Foxtrot one-five, say again'.

'FUCK !!!!!!' said Foxtrot one-five.

'Who?' asked the lass on the radio. getting the laddo's drift.

'The whole fucking lot of them,' he said.

He knew when he said it he was wrong. There was one still standing and every time he said "Fuck" her mouth twitched. He'd met a lass in Benedorm that liked it when he swore. That bitch gave him crabs. He knew not to trust 'em like that any more.

He was right. He looked at his radio and the next thing he knew there was a knitting needle in his bollocks.

'F-U-U-U-U-C-C-C-K-K-KKKKKKKK !!!!!!!' he said.

The biddy blew her top and booted the big spike bollockwards, bloody hard.

The copper didn't need to think. Inside two seconds he had the spike out. Two seconds later the old bitch was buggered and her bum was bleeding badly down the big spike.
'Ooh FUCK !!' she said.

The copper thought about it and wretched into a bucket.

16 - SEX

After a hard night's violence, TYRONE HOODLUM was having a hard time with his woman.

'Give me your head' she said.

He did.

'Mmmmmmmm,' she gobbled. 'There's tasty and hot and hard and that.'

His nuts tightened grimly and his teeth clenched as tight as what his nuts were grim, like. Delicately, her tongue lolled on his tightening and he felt it lightening. She got to the root of the problem and moved up slowly with measured strokes that would satisfy most blokes. Despite himself, TYRONE responded with a few inches and a steady throb that would register on the Richter scale.

'I love a gobfull!' she gasped, surfacing for air.

Whipping out her teeth she nosedived, teasing him with the expert deployment of her gums. A slobber here, a stroke there, a grunt and some dribble on his public hair. TYRONE'S todger touched a tonsil.

TYRONE HOODLUM fought the explosion he could feel taking root. No good. His root exploded.

'Oooh, lovely, lovely!' she dribbled. 'Was it good for you too?'

'Sure,' he grunted, 'thanks Mum.'

17 - FOOD

That night was Friday. The night before had been Thursday and VINCE's money was on the night after being Saturday. Things had a way of happening like that.

She came back from work and got to work in his kitchen. The firm dependability of her magnificent fish-gutting fingers worked backwards into her firmly dependable arms but it was the dependable firmness of her breasts that was firming up his dependable decision making. She would stay, and play, for LIFE!!!!!!!! All he had to do was risk his and, most likely, lose it. His last conscious moment would see him dimly aware that STIG BIG, ELVIS THUG AND TYRONE HOODLUM - THE RAIDERS OF THE LOW FOREHEAD - were jabbing his entrails into his mouth, guffing up a storm and booting his pancreas into oncoming traffic.

Anyone who took them on, bought one, right?

The lass was class, right?

Justice was a stranger in their town and a man's only friend was a smokin' gun. True enough, thought VINCE, he'd witnessed a mean looking Uzi 9 millimetre pistol with a serious shine and a sexy butt puff it's way through twenty Benson's in the pub two nights before.

He was gonna have his hide whipped, guts ripped, entrails tipped and manhood snipped attempting to get his love pump lipped by a class tart until he was an old fart. He had about as much chance of survival as a Mongoose in a meltdown, a batsman in a peltdown, Wembley with the Celts down or a scrawny wimp in a well hard town.

Was he gonna go for it?

He gave her a glance. She had cheekbones like geometry and eyes like sin. An industrial strength work-shirt was ripping under the assault of her apocalyptic jugs, the statuesque firmness of her inner thighs could make the cheapest market stall leggings speak ....and she could cook.

Certain death or not, what was a guy without ambition?

That sorted, he set about sorting the stuff on his plate. What's the point of gravy if a pie can't swim in it? What's the point of baked beans if you can't rip open the top of a pie and pour in a few ? And, what's the point of letting decent gravy slop over the side of a plate when you can build a wall of mashed spuds to soak it up? Add some HP sauce and it's full of force.

VINCE figured she could turn out a meal to put meaning into the life of a wretched tramp festering in a vat of slurry with a boil the size of a grapefruit up his arse. The next time he met a guy in that situation he'd send SHARON into the kitchen to test out the idea.

It was HOT!!!

He forked up some beans. Imbibing the fibre he looked at SHARON and dreamed he was inside her. The HP added that subtle hint of spiciness that fills the world with niceyness. On the first forkfull he'd had a splattering of gravy but, second time around, things got really rich and brown.

SHARON had dissolved the supermarket's granular best to

perfection and the thick creamyness delivered the deep dark secret to his whole being. Smooth, silky and stupendous, the gravy was a bit tremendous. It broke in heated magnificence on his tongue, strong and insistent as it headed throughout his mouth. As the first wave hit his throat the rich and assured aftertaste was announcing itself at the front of his gob. He felt it lingering and delivering after-shocks with a steady pace. He hunted gravy deep into the pie forking up a mixture of bean, pie mince and the precious brown nectar.

This forkfull sent his head spinning as the salty gel of the pie-filling staggered off the sides of his tongue and set to work slopping around the trenches outside his teeth. Half chomped beans turned triple axles as they nosedived into the slop and he hunted around with the tip of his tongue to pull flavour from the murk. Each new tongue-dip provided an orgasm of surprise and spice. The HP was mixing up a treat and every time he stuck in his tongue it took a pointed spicy hit that sent shock waves to the top of his bonce. A few fleeing morsels of bean and minced beef gave up the ghost and slid along his tongue in tasty trails before racing in spirals down his insides sending out waves of warmth that romped round his ribs and left him moaning in stupefied satisfaction.

All that and he hadn't touched his mashed spuds!!!!!!

PUKKA!!!!

18 - VIOLENCE

TYRONE HOODLUM was mad cos he'd been had. Dimly, his imbecilic, in-bred apology for a brain made sense of it. SIR CLEMENT HOODLUM's fondness for thrashing, bashing, mashing and trashing had been directed at DAPHNE in the form of frequent lashings. She'd had it with split lips at hunt balls and anyway, these days, SIR CLEMENT's passions had turned to overseas aid. Aiding in the swift and heartless dispensing of justice.

In kangaroo courts that plumbed hitherto unseen depths of bias, depravity and dick-bonced evidence fabrication, SIR CLEMENT HOODLUM's only problem was which method of unspeakably cruel death to demand as punishment. Given the difficulty of such decisions, SIR CLEMENT had done research. Taking it upon himself to demand front row seats for decapitations, mutilations, floggerations and buggerations the length and breadth of the uncivilized world. No wonder shagging DAPHNE seemed dull when he got home.

DAPHNE for her part had her passions and her pride. Passion-wise she'd have anything. anytime. Pride-wise she couldn't. Leaping on a workman might have offered some randy, uncomplicated, rippling muscled, hard driving, 'ooh push it till it hurts you big man,' gasp gasp, soak the bed, 'bite me, bite me - THERE!!!!!!!, YES - YES - YES, AAaaghhhhh........[massive gulp of air]..... Now fuck off and finish painting my bannisters' solid-sex-action. But it would have caused confusion, shame and a lingering sense of worthlessness in DAPHNE HOODLUM'S mind. So, she took the honourable, sane and worthwhile course of action and rodgererd her only son ragged.

Ragged, rodgered and confused TYRONE HOODLUM considered his lot. He decided he was ragged and rodgered. The rest was too confusing to think about.

Fuck knows, he'd tried it in the family empire. For fully one month he'd assisted in HOODLUM ENEMAS, a division of HOODLUM LTD located in a small corner of the 20 zillion acre HOODLUM estate. TYRONE had worn suits in strange and exiting ways and run around with a clip board. Everyone had agreed he was totally fucking useless.

When he'd asked for a start in farming SIR CLEMENT HOODLUM had thoughtfully kneed his son in the bollocks and announced:
'There's two achers, get going.'
What could a confused fuckwit do, except break heads?

Hell, things could be worse, at least SIR CLEMENT HOODLUM was King Shit of the local lodge and owner of everything local, including the law.

Two heads presented themselves to TYRONE, he broke them. He broke two more within a minute and was punching a short-arse in his short arse when he was spotted.
'You've broken the heads of my garden gnomes and now you're punching one in the bum,' howled a householder, obviously.

'I'm lashing out in a blurred state of hunger and confusion,' tried TYRONE. His probation officer had told him that one would come in useful if people heard it.

In a blurred state of having his gnomes trashed the house-holder was not at all abashed. He grabbed a brush and started to rush. TYRONE HOODLUM met him halfway.
'How do you do?' he said. 'The name's HOODLUM, TYRONE HOODLUM.'

'MENTAL BASTARD!' yelled the householder in his best gutted at losing garden ornaments voice.

'FUCKIN' OFFICIAL!!!!!!!' whispered TYRONE HOODLUM at ear-splitting volume.

Fists and fur flew in a blur as a furious fist-fight began to occur. It occurred with a THWAKKK!!!!!, OOMPHY, URGHH, GRRR, THUD THUD, OHHHYA...FUCK! Later it deviated to a URNGHHH, URNGHHH, HEUCHH, UH,UH, UH before taking a sharp left into ARGHHHHHHHHHHHHHHHH!!!!!!!!!!!!!!!!!!!!!! and coming to a juddering halt with a CRRRNNNNKKKKK.

TYRONE HOODLUM had won, it was as plain as the nose on the householder face which wasn't plain at all 'cos it had spread itself over seven slabs of crazy paving since TYRONE gave it a backheel.

Later, guarding the evidence and waiting for the forensic boys, a policeman came upon the scene. Hell, there was sod all else to do on a lonely evening shift.

19 - SEX

Mouthing her last portion of mash, SHARON started to mouth VINCE. Slowly, sliding a slimy, sliver of tongue, she made him shiver and nearly come. 'Hold on,' she cooed, holding onto his manhood.

The mountainous magnificence of her majestic mammaries mesmerised him as she fondled, felt, drooled and dealt her way - down and down and down and 'OOOOHHHHH, YEAHHHHHHH!!!!!' The alpine-esque assault of her ample assets hung before VINCE like a pair of great tits on an ace bird as she slithered along his stomach and landed on his hummock. Sitting bolt upright, with his lump tucked outasight, she bounced around enough to give him a good night.

Her fingers felt his neck, probing away tensions as her stunning bunning left VINCE humming. Slowly, steadily and with measured timing the timing of their bonking built up slowly, steadily and measuredly.
'I love it slow and steady,' he blurted, trying to sound intelligent but ending up sounding like a bloke who is trying to sound intelligent by talking as he is having mind-blowing sex.

'Don't blurt anything yet!' she teased.

Arching her back in supine splendour she whisked his manhood round like he was in a blender. The rubbing and rubbing and squelchy scrubbing was an experience that was better than going clubbing.

Teasing and squeezing with consummate easing SHARON shimmied in and his head started to spin.

'Now' she whispered, 'just let yourself go.'

He was already on the way. Along several miles of tiny tubes he felt the flood starting to move. Stopping at each gland along the way his load got the same message - 'Ere, son. Take a king-size helping, this is no sordid little wank.'

VINCE tried to hold on to consciousness but the monster blast was cumming fast. Opening his eyes he took in the sweating lissomness of her lustrous flesh and his arriving load took on a warp-drive. This shot packed a recoil that impaled bed springs in his rear end.

The rest was all hazy. Blacking out with an orgasmic shout his mind went weird and roamed about. He had visions of SHARON doing her thing as the room began to spin. Furniture flew and carpet shredded to make a load that he really dreaded. The bed took off as his root exploded and stuff queued up to keep him loaded. In through the crack of his bum and out with a mighty hum came CARPET, BITS OF PLASTER, ALL HIS COPIES OF 'LOADED', TWENTY SEVEN FOOTBALL PROGRAMMES, HIS OLD SCALEXTRIC CAR THAT NEEDED FIXING, HIS TREASURED COPY OF STEVEN WELLS' STORMING BOOK 'TITS-OUT TEENAGE TERROR TOTTY' AND A PICTURE OF VINCE AS A BABY.

Eventually, he ejaculated the whole room, street and the entire known universe up to and including the stars in Orion's belt. The mighty pump ripped his lump. It had a sound like working drag line attacking a carelessly abandoned lawnmower as a fishing boat sinks in a nearby lake and a hopeless thrash metal band jam inside a cowshed. Not exactly the sort of sound you'd hear everyday.

VINCE opened his eyes expecting to see SHARON rattling, ragged and dribbling a roomful. Instead she was panting, glancing and leaking a spoonful.

'OOOOOHHHHHHHHhhhhhhhhhh!!!!!!' he sighed in general ecstasy. Not only had he experienced mind-altering sex of unutterably pleasurable dimensions. He had also registered that his room was intact and so his Mum wouldn't blow her top about his pumping a portion of his pad into a bird he hardly knew. You know how Mums can be.

'So,' he pontificated pointlessly, 'tell me, SHARON, have there been any blokes before me?'

Later, she said: 'I'm off to see my Dad and little brother in jail tomorrow, fancy coming?'

'Thanks,' he wigged, 'I just did.'

20 - FOOD

Predictably, VINCE went along for the ride. In VINCE's mind the words SHARON and 'ride' had undergone a magical fusion only understood by those few who have taken the basic sex act into dimensions uncharted by the mechanical pumping of the porn industry and the endless meandering drivel of hand-knitted new agers intent on pontificating about spiritual love on the strength of their first hand shandy.

He wanted so much to tell her how deep it all went for him. To share the unique gift of their love. Shuffling through the desolate gates of the desultory prison VINCE looked deep into SHARON's eyes and began to speak his mind.

'SHARON,' he sighed softly, never taking his eyes from hers. Then he walked smack into a wall, bounced off and forgot what the fuck he was on about.

Later, SHARON and VINCE took their seats in the waiting-room. In walked MR GOER and SHAZ's brother, LITTLE JOHNNY GOER. VINCE noticed her Dad was older than her brother, that got him thinking. Their prison clothes were ON. So were their prison hair-cuts. Both of them were wearing prison boots. Their boots were ON!!

'It's rough in here for innocent men,' opened Mr GOER predictably. 'Daily blokes are buggered, spat upon, beaten and biffed and I'll be buggered if I can figure out why.'

'Then don't figure out why,' volcanoed VINCE, reasonably.

52

'I won't,' said her Dad, 'but it still buggers my concentration when there's a bloke on my cellmate and I'm trying to watch EMMERDALE.'.

'Hey, SHARON, is this bloke giving you the odd poke?' fragged her brother fraternally, gesturing at VINCE.

'There's nothing odd about it,' VINCE dangled defensively.

'Come on,' frittered LITTLE JOHNNY, 'all some blokes wanna do is lie in the rank sweat of an enseamed bed, stewed in corruption, honeying and making love over the nasty sty.'

'What's it to you?' VINCE howled heroically. 'I've had some great holidays with Club 18-30 and that's FUCKIN' OFFICIAL!!!!!'

Jutting gigantically, SHARON shrugged.
'This bloke is so gone on me gobblograms he's gonna risk his life in a totally futile attempt to get you sprung. I told him I'd TASTE THE PASTE for a good long bit to get the two of you out of the shit.'

'No shit?' doodled her Dad in a fatherly fashion.

'There will be when STIG BIG, TYRONE HOODLUM AND ELVIS TWAT have finished with the poor wanker' butted her brother in a brotherly fashion.

'You two are fashion victims,' SHARON shrugged. Then she pulled out a WALNUT WHIP all round.

The peak-like pretensions of the sweet with small dimensions hid a world of taste that most people never mention.
'This is a treat from a chocolate shop that's light and fluffy and with goodness on top,' she cackled commercially.
Surveying the sloping side, her brother added:
'Above all else, it's healthy.' He pointed to the ample walnut on top to add weight to his point.

'Keep yer point outasight, son,' said his Dad, sensibly. 'There's bull queers in here that hold such things, dear.'

'Thanks Ducky, I'll remember that,' LITTLE JOHNNY minced, majestically.

'Just fancy that,' figged SHARON, 'our Dad and brother quaffing like queens.' And they were, tonguing the walnuts to perfection.

Wincing visibly, SHARON delivered the facts with admirable accuracy.

'Consider the seriously underrated WALNUT WHIP,' she opened, 'that summit seething with vitamins and fibre held up by matchless chocolate. With the strength to deliver a taste punch and yet delicate enough to fracture gently, revealing the light and fluffy sweetness beneath. Each fleeting taste an unpredictable delight of creamy perfection and solid, splendid chocolate. Those gentle ridges melting away to nothing as you hold the exquisite chocolatty charms in the secret, solitary splendour of your mouth.' Then she sighed orgasmically.

'Yeah,' VINCE agreed, 'It's the twist in the tail that never fails. Your mind says it's gone but the bottom lingers on. The final little roundy totally astounds me. Because the little circle base always packs the taste.'

And it did.

Instantly LITTLE JOHNNY GOER did a back flip over his chair. Dipping one foot in a cleaner's bucket, he proceeded to rip out a light bulb, stick a finger in the socket and sprout an afro. The smell of burning flesh exploded into every nostril within fifty yards as his involuntary ticks and jerks sent his tongue in and out of his gob one hundred times a minute. Forcing his free hand to his mouth he positioned his WALNUT WHIP and totally tongued the top. Dropping to his knees he slid the chocolate mini-mountain into the mouth of a passing bloke. Sticking a straw in the bloke's ear and sucking off the sweet splendour, using the bloke's gob as a sort of blender.

Walnut Whips, how do you eat yours?

Later, her Dad said to VINCE: 'Me and SHAZ and her brother want to talk family stuff. Why don't you fuck off, you puff. Incidentally, next week me piles need sorting in the prison hospital.'

'Never mind Dad,' spluttered Sharon, 'I'm sure the doctors here are very good.'

21 - VIOLENCE

SHARON was still wigging it with her old man and VINCE had time to kill. Prisons ain't famous for their abundant leisure facilities but let's give this lot their due. In the interests of the warder's annual sex-tourism outing to Far East Sleaze Ghetto Heaven, they were blagging a few quid selling tickets to operations in the prison hospital. VINCE bought that ticket and he took that ride.

In front of him on the slimy wooden benches were a knitting granny, two spikey haired sickos with a glue habit, a vicar in Kickers, a sheep asleep and a bloke with a hard on who worked in a garden.
Hey, it takes all sorts.

The poster announced:
"Carver and the Goblin tackling a guy with gallstones."

No shit? VINCE thought it was an execution.

'Dumb-shit, meathead, motherfuck bastard!' spat Carver. 'If this asshole bleeds anywhere near my sneakers again I'll pour battery acid in his eyeballs till his brains are comin' out of his ears like fuckin' porridge.'

'Hoo hoo hoo,' chuckled his stumpy companion, round shoulders bobbing up and down either side of his piggy head. 'I just love it when you get mad 'cos that's when the real carving starts, hoo hoo hoo.'

'Shut the fuck up you goblin and give me a bread knife,' said Carver.

'That lil' scalpel you got cuts real clean and neat,' said The Goblin, unable to shut the fuck up.

'Yeah but the fucking bread knife is quicker.' Carver followed the bread knife with his clenched fist, thrusting it into the gaping body cavity before him. 'Come on you fucker,' he grunted. The immobile lump of meat on the table jerked at the violation.

'I rate a good cutting when I've got my elbows into 'em,' said Carver stumbling towards intelligence.

'Hoo hoo hoo,' gurgled The Goblin, 'I can get in to my shoulders, hoo hoo hoo.'

'That's because you're a short arsed, stump-armed apology for a life form. Get real, you creep. Who else would give you a job?'

'Hoo hoo hoo,' hooed The Goblin, 'I don't care shit about none of that because I love it fine here with you. Look out, he's gonna blow!'

The slob on the slab spouted blood.
'Shit,' cursed Carver crudely stemming the flow.

'He's gonna be a real mess when you're through, hoo hoo hoo,' said the stump with the goblin grin.

'He knew the score,' said Carver grunting as he slapped on a rusty arterial clamp. 'Wise up you retard. If this guy cared shit about his looks he'd never have got himself jailed and thrown himself on the mercy of a PRISON HOSPITAL.'

These dispensers of heartless death would do for SHARON's old man in seconds, and that would leave VINCE done for. Heroically, VINCE thought only of SHARON and the stuff she could with her hips and lips. If her old man wasn't out NOW!!, VINCE's luck was out for life.

22 - SEX

TYRONE HOODLUM celebrated the gnome-trashing with LAGER!!! Seven pints in the snug of the MINER'S SPUTUM was followed by a session swilling the fermented sweat of a battery pig in the Smoke Room of the SHEEP AND CONDOM. Later he could be found ranting in his cups as he quaffed raw testosterone in the public bar of the STOMACH PUMPER'S ARMS.

'That'll put lead in yer pencil, Laddie,' blurted the barman.

'Shame,' shrugged TYRONE, 'I was hopin' it'd put sperm in me penis.'

Calling out cachophonously for companionship as he swilled fresh bum-boil pus in the ALE STRANGLERS BRAIN CELL, TYRONE HOODLUM drew a mob and spewed from his gob. Retching into the shag pile with rhythmic abundance, he puked, howled, quivered and scowled himself into a pungent pile.

'He's puked on my haemorrhoids,' stated a bloke, 'I'm gonna do 'im.'

'That's the demented offspring of SIR CLEMENT HOOD-LUM and you'll do him at your peril,' brandished the barman.

'Uh, yeah,' agreed TYRONE, intelligently.

Just then PLOD erupted into the pub, mob handed. 'This is a bloke's nose,' stated one waving a splintered mess. 'And we're looking for a back-heeling bastard covered in gnome-plaster.'

'He's it,' punted the pile man, pointing at TYRONE.

And he was.

Later, TYRONE awoke in a general stupor. Feeling unwell and clocking a cell.

Shit, he spat.

'I hope you floss before you snog,' recycled a copper.

Shit, spat TYRONE again.

'Cut it you wag, I've done the gag,' postured the pig.

'What's the score?' grunted TYRONE.

'Psycho 1 Plod 1,' cackled the cop.

'In your fuckin' dreams, Rozzer,' ranted TYRONE, reasonably. 'I'm the son of.....'

'The bloke that's away hanging the third world for lookin' at each other's pints.'

Shit, spat TYRONE.

'You stupid twat, we've just done that.'

This was serious. SIR CLEMENT HOODLUM had only last week been called upon to put several double parking offenders to the rusty sword, cat o' nine tails and soldier ants under the foreskin. He would be away for weeks. The cops knew it, TYRONE knew it, and before he could get out of this sorry mess he'd have to face her in the dress. Oh shit, she'd just arrived.

Cynthia Pemberton-Slag loved probation with passion. Which was tight really cos she didn't show much passion about anything else. Daily she took it upon herself to bring rays of culture, and worse, into the blighted biographies of hardened and hopeless petty criminals. It was the hardened bit she liked. Those rippling manly chests pushing grimy vests were, for her, the best. The cops left her to it, bastards that they were. Her style never wavered. She'd make 'em read, grab a crotch and knead, then drain a shot of seed. To put it another way, she was up for forcing the criminally stupid to read pointless books before preying on the same sex-starved specimens by touching them up and then letting them up her. It might have been sordid but what other perks were there for a fat lass with no personality and a job in probation?

Totally testosteroned, TYRONE tingled with trepidation.

From a distance she looked like a water filled cement bag in a dress with a severed bull-dog's head thrown on top. Up close she was just plain PIG UGLY.

'Now then dear,' she whispered in his ear, as she came near, so he could hear. 'Did you think any-more about that little couplet we had last time?'

He'd thought about nothing else for the following week. The poetry she read made his head hurt. To get her out he'd given her a squirt. Pumping away with grim insistence he was bloody amazed he'd gone the distance.

'Listen,' he lumbered, 'I know we had a bit of a shag...'

'Rhyming couplets, TYRONE. I was talking about those words I read you.'

Oh shit, this heartless bitch was gonna get him READING!!!!!

'Remember?,' she rumbled, reading aloud. 'When a man is tired of London, he is tired of life.'

'Yeah,' he yelped. 'So how come people going home from work don't drop dead on tube trains all the time?' he added with stunning insight.

'Ooh TYRONE,' she gushed.

TYRONE examined the gush staining the cell floor. UGHHH!!!!

'It's about culture, dear,' she dribbled. The dribble joined the gush and TYRONE's legs turned to mush. 'The man behind this thought about his history. Everything that London meant. Couldn't you put your feelings into words like that? Feelings about your home, what it means. Something to give you a sense of well-being and move you away from crime.'

'No,' he stated, obviously.

'Try, try, oh, just let it flow.'

TYRONE watched as she let it flow, then he retched, and had a go. 'When a man is tired of London, then he is tired of life,' he opened.

'Go on,' she gurgled, opening a little more.

'And when a man is tired of Cleator Moor, he's only tired of shite....In my opinion at least.'

TYRONE was trying, very trying. But the one-woman, wobbling, PIG UGLY apology for a probation officer set her standards lower than a terminally ill tramp with his last fleeting hard on.

'OOOOOHHHHH!!!!!, TYRONE!' she dribbled abundantly. 'Take me, shake me, make me know it. I can give myself, only to a poet.'

Shit, spat TYRONE.

'Cut the wank, we've had that prank,' Piped a passing PLOD.

Then he said, 'Yesterday there was a pile of stunned pensioners and dead pigs, suspicion falls on you, ELVIS and STIG.' He threw in a note about pensioners and parliaments. 'Recognize the writing, TYRONE?' he grinned.

Things were SERIOUS!!!!!!!

Not only had TYRONE butted, gutted and nutted his way into serious shit. He was also in over his challenged head now the note had been read. 'Plod 1 Psycho 1.....FUCK!' he roared, defiantly.

'Oh, yes you smooth talker!' slobbered Cynthia. 'I'll just slip out in the corner, do what you want to me.'

Briefly, TYRONE HOODLUM, decided that he wanted to gut her ample insides and slip out of the police station in her pelt. Sensibly, he realised that the deluge of blubber alone would drown him.

He thought, then he thought, by the time he'd thought again he was almost thinking. Then he did something.

Facing him with the figure of a warthog with a taste for deep fried Mars Bars, Cynthia grunted:
'Do your thing, TYRONE. Release your inner sexual desire.'

'Thanks,' he spat sexily, wiping his rear end on a pillowcase, 'I did. I've just had a shit in your handbag.'

GUTTED!!!!!!!!!!!!

23 - FOOD

Still spewing inside after clocking the insides of the poor
labbed sod in the prison VINCE felt like nowt by mouth, except hers.

'I'm up for a stuffin,' slobbered SHARON.

'Yer muffin or yer belly?' he mumbled romantically.

'Fuck me,' she flirted, flirtatiously.

VINCE was lining up his approach run when she went on:
'That's ELVIS TWAT is that. He's up to no good and he's
earchin' for food.'

She was right, ELVIS was TWATTING his way along the
avement and holding his head high. It had been somebody else's head
o start with but hanging by the hair and dripping in the street, it was
caring the honest, God-fearing folks up a treat.

A tramp tramped up.
'Give us some head will yer,' he cackled cannibalistically.

'ELVIS TWAT gives head to no man,' emphasised ELVIS,
ccurately.

'I suppose you're just gonna set me on fire like all the others,' talked the tramp.

'Nah, I'm starvin' and that's FUCKIN' OFFICIAL!!!!!'

'How about having an Indian?' rumbled the tramp reasonably
'That one over there has a reputation.'

ELVIS clocked the sign.
"The Bulimic Bengali - Ringpiece Roasters a speciality."

SHAZ and VINCE watched from a distance as ELVIS entered
Then she said:
'That TWAT doesn't know us. Let's get in and watch him. We
might learn something that'll get me gobbling you till our lives are
through.'

ELVIS was inside, VINCE was heading that way, then he
heard a Bengali out the back say:
'We're running out of minced beef, the situation is causing
grief and the van ain't due for an hour or two.'

'Ah fuck it,' said his mate resourcefully, 'slip that cannibal
tramp a laxative, catch the results in a bucket and slap in enough curry
paste to kill the fetid taste.'
Then he added, tasteful:
'Them inside won't know the difference anyway.'

Them inside the Bulimic Bengali were ELVIS TWAT, a
knitting granny, two spiky haired sickos with a glue habit, a vicar in
Kickers, a sheep asleep and a man with a hard on who worked in a
garden.
Hey, it takes all sorts, in all sorts of places.
VINCE and SHARON started shuffling in too.

'So what's with the Bulimic Bengali tag?' rumbled the
reverend in the fashionable footwear, reverently.

'Bulimic is when you want it out as soon as it's in so you can
get all the taste and stay quite thin,' waffled a waiter. 'All our dishes fill

hat wish. Just ask the geezer coming out the bog.'

A bloodshot skeleton with steaming wellingtons shuffled in looking thin. 'That there is Luciano Pavarotti and that's real steam rising' from his botty,' the waiter lied monumentally. 'He may well appear to have lost a few pounds, but when his ring-piece roasts he can still make a sound.'

Rumbling into SHARON's ear, VINCE spelled it out about the meat, tramp and curry paste. Then he laid it on thick about what that lot might do to somebody's insides. She thought, and she thought, and by the time she'd thought some more she had come up with a thoughtful retort.

'Bulimic Bengali is an understatement, these innocent people will be spilling out of their sphincters so bad they should re-name this place 'The Fucking Disgrace.'

She had a point, she had two, hell, VINCE loved it when her nipples stood out like THAT!!!!

SHAZ and VINCE ordered cokes and crisps, pointing out the packets they wanted and keeping them in sight all the way to the table. ELVIS TWAT was in a hurry and VINCE was glad when he ordered Vindaloo Curry.

Peering through a window crack, VINCE clocked the tramp and the bucket out the back.
'I'm not well, you know,' talked the tramp.
Blasting into the bucket, the tramp shouted 'FUCK IT!!!!!!!'
Bog-eyed and blazing his dump was amazing.
'ARGHHHHH!!!!!!!!!!!!!,' he whispered, laxatived into a looseness that left him collapsed and useless.
'Oooohhhhhhhhhhhh ughhhhhhh, ug,' he collapsed in general squalor and despair.

VINCE's mind got to figuring, twenty feet away, ELVIS TWAT was laying into mango chutney with a manly relish. His strong stomach was part of a strong image based on strong acts of mindless violence. VINCE figured he was quite strong. But the apocalyptic assault of the curry paste and crap was going to put the blast furnace guts of ELVIS TWAT under serious pressure. If VINCE was gonna

65

make a move on this moron, this was his best chance.

'If you're gonna make a move on this moron, this is your bes chance,' shimmied SHARON, crisps crunching in her gob.

'Yeah,' VINCE grunted.

Clocking the Vic in the in Kicks, VINCE whispered to him:
'Take my word for it, pal. If you know what's good for you you'll order vegetarian and give this joint a wide one in future. Pass the word to the others, but don't bother with that evil looking TWAT!! in the corner.'

So, in the beginning was the word and the word was with the Vicar in Kickers. Within five minutes the word was also with a knitting granny, two spiky haired sickos with a glue habit, a sheep asleep and a man with a hard on who worked in a garden. They all ordered veggie.

VINCE went to the bog to drop a log. All this squalor was doing for his insides. VINCE thought about ELVIS TWAT's insides. Hi own insides took a turn for the worse. He got out the worst in one soli burst. Things felt better. When he went back to the Bulimic Bengali, the whispering campaign still had free reign.

'What's the word,' grunted ELVIS loudly, clocking the conversation going round.

'I was just saying you can't beat a good shit,' VINCE lied mightily.

'No,' carped the Vic in Kicks, 'but in certain circumstances you could boil it.'

'MMMMMM,' mmmm-ed the granny, 'I suppose a good bread knife would take slices, but in my long experience of life you definitely can't beat a good shit.'

'You could toast it,' spewed the spiky sickos. But by the time you'd got it cooked the toast would be well fucked. Anyway, in our long experienced of spiky haired sicko stunts, it is our considered opinion that you can't beat a good shit.'

'You lot are talking crap,' rapped ELVIS TWAT, specifically.

'And since you're all ordering veggie I'm having extra helpings of this powerful and manly minced beef Vindaloo, NOW!!!!! And since I'm as hard as nails and that's FUCKING OFFICIAL, I'm not paying more than a crisp TENNER.'

That one got the waiter mad, and he gave ELVIS TWAT everything he had. The fetid stench of curried crap filled the joint and caused a flap. The massive pile looked quite vile till ELVIS TWAT swilled it flat. The festering slop entered ELVIS in dribbling fork fulls that left SHARON stemming a retch. Somewhere in the stinking pool was an apology for a helping of rice and about three tons of throat-tripping, industrial strength curry paste. ELVIS acted the manly TWAT to perfection, chomping it down with a laugh and a lager.

'He's packing a pound of a tramp's log, I could jump him in the bog.' VINCE suggested bravely.

'That TWAT has a strength beyond belief, such a move would end in grief,' shuffled SHARON.

She was right. ELVIS' guts were working overtime on the curried and fetid slime. His stomach heaved, then heaved some more as his mighty frame paced the floor.

The assembled staff of the Bulimic joint were just starting to get the point.

'I am ELVIS TWAT!!!!,' roared the man mountain, honestly. 'And I think that beef vindaloo was CRAP!'

Shit, spat a waiter.

'Ooh neat, another repeat,' ooh-ed SHARON.

'It was crap, complete crap,' urged Elvis.

'Nah,' grunted the waiter. 'There was some curry paste, and a few sultanas. We might be cut price but we're not total 'nanas.'

The chef arrived, looking sheepish. In fact, he looked very sheepish. That is sheepish as in not exactly human. The sheep asleep woke up. 'How the fuck did you get a chef's job in this joint?' asked the sheep that used to be asleep. 'The last time I saw you you were chewin the cud and going on the odd ram raid.'

Shit, spat ELVIS.

'Ooh, I'm in Heaven, that's number seven,' ooh-ed SHARON

Just then, ELVIS TWAT roared in annoyance, defiance and the appliance of science. 'I AM ELVIS TWAT. I MIGHT HAVE BEEN TAKEN FOR A TOTAL MUG, BUT WHEN I'M PISSED OFF I CAN BE A RIGHT THUG. OFFICIAL!!!!!!'

24 - VIOLENCE

ELVIS TWAT had been crapped and curried in the cynical
ursuit of cash. Waving a TENNER defiantly he defied anyone to take
: off him.

'I AM ELVIS TWAT. I MIGHT HAVE BEEN TAKEN FOR A
'OTAL MUG, BUT WHEN I'M PISSED OFF I CAN BE A RIGHT
'HUG,' he cackled for the sake of continuity. 'If you lot think that I'm
arting with a TENNER for that curried crap pile, you can think
gain.'

The staff thought again.

'Okay, call it eight quid,' said one, thoughtfully.

'I AM ELVIS TWAT. I MIGHT HAVE BEEN TAKEN FOR
.....'

'Yeah, yeah, get on with it,' grunted a waiter.

'If you lot think that I'm parting with EIGHT QUID for that
rried crap pile, you can think again.'

The staff thought again.

'Seven fifty, can't say fairer than that,' said one thoughtfully.

Shit, spat ELVIS.

'Ooh great, it's number eight,' ooh-ed SHARON.

Just then the action moved on as one liners were trashed in the interests of adding some serious VIOLENCE!!!!!!

Butting a Bengali in the buttocks ELVIS TWAT hurled him hard into a menu card. Ripping into a waiter with rhythmic aggression ELVIS grabbed his tongue. Which was tight really cos he'd ripped into the bloke through his rear end. Pulling him inside out with a single stroke ELVIS splattered intestines over acres of wall.
   'Fuckin' great,' mumbled the TWAT, 'Now we've got some paste up, let's wallpaper this joint.'

In the next five minutes ELVIS TWAT flayed a waiter alive,

'That's for trying to skin me,' he howled in a hopeless attempt at humour. As he broke bones and pulped a pelvis, the victory all belonged to ELVIS. The Bulimic Bengali was wallpapered with bits of bulimic Bengali.

Huddled in a corner with the knitting granny, vicar in Kickers and the rest, VINCE marvelled at the manly power packed into the TWAT's frame and figured following him had been a bad idea.

'You whispering bastards are next,' he attacked.

Just then, the Vindaloo got through.

'ARGHHH!!!!!!!,' screamed ELVIS collapsing like a brutal thug in a story in which brutal thugs get brutal and then collapse at the moment when they might attack an important character and bring the whole thing to an end before the end, sort of thing.

'ARGHHHH!!!!!!!'

'ARGHHHH!!!!!!!'

'ARGHHHH!!!!!!!'

'He's trying to tell us something,' twigged the granny. 'What are you trying to tell us, dear?'

'ARGHHHH!!!!!!!'

'He's trying to tell us, ARGHHHH!!!!!!!' she added, accurately.

'We should make a bolt for it,' VINCE blubbered bravely to SHARON.

'A bolt?,' she figged. 'A cement casing wouldn't contain the eruption that's gonna spew from his guts.'

She was right, the serious heat of the Vindaloo had cut the crap and broken through.

'He's being internally incinerated by strong curry used as a masking agent on the slurry,' VINCE spurted scientifically.

With compassion, the granny grinned at ELVIS.
'Are you burnin,' love?' she blurted.

And he was. The violence he had single handedly administered to the Bulimic Bengalis was nothing compared to the immense assault of curry and slurry that hit his insides, causing lots of worry.

The chef who had missed out on a mauling and still looked sheepish announced:
'I'm away back to the cud and ram raiding.'
Looking at the sheep that used to be asleep the chef-sheep added:
'You know, I miss those carfree ram raids. What was it we sang as we headed for the rams to get impregnated with lambs?'
The chef-sheep and the sheep asleep that was now awake looked into each others eyes as they recalled the phrase from those far off days. Together they screamed....LET'S GET THE FLOCK OUT OF

HERE!'

They flocked out, leaving ELVIS to collapse in agony with added pain, disgrace, torture and general discomfort. Bravely taking up a position behind a wall of dustbins in a bus shelter VINCE made a heroic phone call asking about the price of hiring an armoured car and waited for ELVIS TWAT to emerge.

He did holding his head up high. The tramp tramped up.
'Give us some head will yer,' he cackled cannibalistically.

'ELVIS TWAT gives head to no ....oh, fuckin' hell, have it. My raging guts are burnin' up.' He tossed the head, which was just about the most repulsive sex act VINCE had ever seen, since the thing was going green.

Grabbing the hurled head, the tramp said:
'Yummy, dinner!'
Diving in, he fixed ELVIS with a grin and slowly started to talk. 'You know,' he said. 'You know...,' at this point it was obvious he had a slow and determined tone to his voice. The kind of tone that leads you to realise that he was about to make his most important contribution of the story. The sort of tone that suggests a minor character is going to throw in a nugget of wisdom or a little ironic twist. The kind of tone that might lead someone following the story to realise that this little cameo part was being played by an actor, well known comedian or some other celebrity out to expand his portfolio of work.
'You know,' said the tramp who was now milking his moment by throwing in thoughtful silences and totally needless repetitions of one simple phrase, 'You know.'

'Fucking get on with it!' rumbled ELVIS, reasonably.

'Well, you really would have been better off setting me on fire. Because, as it turned out, in a roundabout way, I got to set you on fire. Now, what are the chances of that happening, eh?'

Shit, spat Elvis.

'Ooh, that's fine, it's number nine,' ooh-ed SHARON.

25 - SEX

Grunting gormlessly at the bar of The Flapping Penis, STIG BIG piled into his fifteenth pint. He was thinking. The smell of burning wood hung in the air. The barman knew STIG was in speculating form because he'd managed the walk from the door without his knuckles once touching the floor. Hammering that Herdwick with a pork torpedo had brought a new depth to STIG's dense head.

'Giz it,' gassed the barman.

'Uh?' uh-ed STIG, predictably.

'What yer thinkin', STIG?'

'Well, yer know that moment when yer gonna shoot yer load, like? When it ain't out but it's on the way, and yer just know yer gonna cum?'

'Yeah, what about it, STIG?'

'Fuckin' magic.'

'Yeah .....and?'

'It's magic, fuckin' good.'

'Sure, STIG,' surged the barman twigging the time was up on this talk. He knew the score on humouring STIG. The BIG lad might earn precisely nowt much shovelling shit and cleaning tractors up at the farm but he spent twice that every time he came through the door to quaff ale. Thick as the shit he shovelled, STIG delivered mighty thoughts slowly. It was a smart move to support him and get out of the conversation sometime around the second sentence.

Behind him in the snug a bloke surged.
'Whaddya you know, STIG? You've never had it with a lass.'

'I have too,' STIG howled heroically.

'What? You've spewed yer sack right up a crack?'

'Uh?' uh-ed STIG, predictably.

'Don't confuse him,' cackled the barman knowing that the sagging meathead on the stool could quaff the assembled snug under the table. STIG might be a moron with a psychopathic relish of raw meat and rough action but - fuck it - he paid cash and drank like a camel with a hole in it's hump. A solid punter is a solid punter, right?

'Tell us,' spluttered the snug, 'What was it like with a lass, STIG?'

'Rough, she grabbed me tackle and rubbed it a bit. She moved her hand up and down and that.'

'Yeah.....and?'

'Well, that's what it was like.'

'So, STIG,' spluttered the snug some more, 'did you give her a right good pummelling?'

'Aye.'

'TELL US, YOU STUPID TWAT!' roared the pub, reasonably.

'She's rubbing me,' spoke STIG, 'like all slow and that, and she's muttering summat about liking a man big and hard. But I tell yer, there was nowt happenin'.' You could get a tighter hold on a turd than she had on me tackle.'

'DID YOU TELL HER, STIG?' spewed the snug.

'Fuckin' did an all,' blurted the BIG lad. 'She's rubbin me and that and I says 'Oh fer fuck's sake get a grip.' I elbowed her off the couch, got a decent grip and did the bloody job meself. Lasses, man, they know nowt about pleasing a bloke.'

'I thought you said you pummelled her?' mumbled a man.

'Aye, but what's that got to do with shagging?' queried STIG, simply.

Sensing sport and not clocking the danger, into the banter came a lady stranger. 'You look like a bloke that likes to nosh,' she boshed, surveying the basic ruggedness of STIG's basically rugged frame. So, do you ever get in with a lass and go down for the gravy?'

'Uh?' uh-ed STIG, predictably.

'You see, STIG,' staggered the stranger with no sense of danger, 'lasses give you what you want when you give 'em a bit of what they want. A lass loves to be eaten. You know, get your head between her legs and eat her a bit. A bloke with a tongue and a jaw like yours, could lick up a lass to a round of applause.'

Just then, STIG erupted up her skirt, chomping, whamping, slurping, burping, beefing and teething. He got some gravy and a slice of meat before the pub dragged him off and put him back on his feet.

'Never mind,' mumbled the barman taping a slice of flesh back onto the lasses' leg and hardly figging as he called an ambulance, 'it's amazing how well they can stitch 'em back in hospital these days.'

'What's the fuckin' bother?' fragged STIG, furtively, 'Lasses love being eaten. That one just said so.'

'Sure, STIG,' surged the snug, spewing a bit.

Later, when they'd all cleaned up the mess and that, STIG surged into his seventeenth pint and grunted, 'You know that moment, when yer just know you're gonna cum......fuckin' magic.'

26 - FOOD

TYRONE HOODLUM was getting looks. Her in the dress was not too impressed with the turd in the handbag trick. The cops had left them in the cell figuring that she'd be milking TYRONE'S CROTCH CONKERS into submission and doing untold damage to his mental stability. It might be cruelty beyond belief but - hell - it saved them losing limbs steaming into him and pushing their limited brains to try and knacker his limited brain. He'd tried hammering hard on the door and begging for help but PLOD just shouted 'Get in there my Son' and left him.

The total cruelty and abandonment surprised TYRONE. In the interests of justice he'd got the odd bit of probation after committing cold-blooded murder, even the son of SIR CLEMENT HOODLUM had to be seen to be within the law. But this time PLOD outside seemed seriously confident. Okay, it might be his handwriting on the note, and maybe he had killed the local constabulary a bit, but...

'Oi, you wanker PLODS, us doin' for the other shift just gives you lot a better chance of making sarge, dunnit?'

'What was that TYRONE?' spat a passing PLOD.
'Sounded suspiciously like a confession to me.'

Shit, it was. 'Je ne regret nowt,' spat TYRONE internationally. Backpedaling as furiously as defender Mike Graham faced by tricky opposing strikers the year Carlisle United finished bottom of fucking everything. He was gonna have to think. Hell, he knew that was beyond him. He was gonna have to sit it out till PLOD figured he'd have enough time in there with her in the fucking dress, then his Mum would spring him.

The last time she'd come down to pick him up his fingers had ended up smelling like fish for a week, what was 'ovary tickling' any-way?' Whatever it was it gave him a rash on his elbow. Still, it was better than getting in with the lawyer who asked him questions that made his head hurt. Given the way PLOD were pontificating outside, it sounded like he'd need the lawyer. But he could save that for court and lay himself in a few splatter comics from HOODLUM PUBLICA-TIONS for when the lawyer guy did his long speech and got TYRONE off.

Worse, much worse, he was fucking starvin!!!!!!'

Her in the dress was surly and giving him glares. Her hefty hulk needed food too. There was a difference. She'd brought some. It takes a desperate situation to make Pringles exciting but TYRONE HOOD-LUM had passed desperate around the same time his rear end and the pillowcase made contact. She slid the Pringles from her shopping bag and moved them slowly between the elephantine expanse of her legs. For a second TYRONE figured the mighty tube was about to see service as a make-shift todger.

'You've hurt me more deeply than you know,' yelped the Pemberton-Slag, 'So I want you to know that any attempt to get at these Pringles will be met with their disappearance into the one hole you refuse to visit,' she added, skilfully.

Uncorking the cap she removed the circular snack that melts with a crack. The lightly-salted smooth taste melted to a paste. Each Pringle adding a tingle and slowly blending into the never ending satisfying mulch of munchy magnificence. Holding one up to the shaft of light from the barred window Cynthia Pemberton-Slag reached for the superlatives.

'Clear and crisp and even, wouldn't you say TYRONE?' she mumbled with a moan and a passing reference to a Christmas carol.

'Share 'em or I'll kill yer,' he retorted.

'And leave PLOD out there with enough evidence to put you away? I don't think so. I'll just put away a few more Pringles.'

She did. The chomped mulch was now forming ridges within her teeth, spreading to the sides of her mouth and rubbing a little but still the assault continued.

'They're light and round and cost less than a pound,' sighed Cynthia. They were, as the mid-packet sensation arrived, Cynthia slowed to savouring pace. The light saltiness had done its work and now she gazed longingly at the tube, waiting for each linger of flavour in her mouth to remind her brain of the cunning longevity of the simple snack. She crunched down on a round edge and felt the flakes spilling into her. She marvelled at the scientific brilliance of snack man-ufacturers who had created a crisp experience that delivered crunching and munching with none of the stinging and scraping that a rogue thick crisp can dump on the unsuspecting punter.

Dependable to the very last, the Pringles were still in there, salting her tongue and teasing her taste buds as the tube rattled in emptiness.

'Aaaaahhhhhhh!!!!!!', sighed the Slag leaning into the cell wall. 'There's a little tingle, in every Pringle.'

'Fuck,' spat TYRONE. 'There's a whole twat nation working in probation.'

27 - VIOLENCE

That night was Saturday, the night before had been Friday and the night after was going to be Sunday. Things had a way of happening like that in those days.

The Prison Officers were locking 'em in for the night. They were also breaking the news.

'The clocks go forward tonight,' they said, accurately.

'Since many of you bastards are locked up twenty three hours a day and tomorrow is a twenty three hour day you lot are basically, fucked 'till the day after,' they added, reasonably.

'But that's more incarceration and torture than a man can bear,' added LITTLE JOHNNY GOER, drawing deeply on his reserves of innocence and injustice.

'Hang on to them reserves,' advised a screw. 'You'll need 'em to sustain you through two days of being locked in with a bloke up your cell-mate.'

It was true. The bloke was already up and clearly planning to stay.

'This is fucking outrageous!' jutted LITTLE JOHNNY.

'It's fucking,' agreed a prison officer clocking the bottom action on the bottom bunk, 'but if you want to talk about outrageous, you should have seen that home made dildo with a toothbrush end we pulled out of a dead bloke's back-bits last week. His back bits were.......

'Rectum,' corrected JOHNNY, medically. 'Them back-bits are called a RECTUM.'

'Yeah, well it didn't do him any good.'

BOOM BOOM!!!!!!!!

The doors were closing along the landing.

'So, anyway,' spurted the screw, 'for one day only you lot were supposed to have your exercise between 3 and 4 in the morning as a special treat. Ain't our fault that the government have decided to abolish three o' clock. You could do something about it if you had votes. Whaddya know, life's shite eh?', he added sympathetically.

And it was.

The bloke up the cell mate was pumping and grunting. Later he changed to grunting and pumping, then they changed round. LITTLE JOHNNY's cell-mate started pumping and grunting. Then he did some grunting and pumping. Stopping for baby oil and bit of mutual mastur- bation, they started pummelling, porking, shafting and grafting.

In his rattling bunk, JOHNNY was rattling.

'Can't you sods keep it down?' he shouted reasonably. 'Some of us in here are trying to sleep.'

'Can't keep it down,' grunted the bunker below. 'I'm sticking up for me Dad, cos he stuck up for me,' he added, throwing in an unexpected reference to reproduction.

Johnny gave it a glare. True enough. His cell mate - 'Dense' Donny Fraser was indeed rodgering his own Dad - 'Dense' Donny Fraser Sr.

Just then LITTLE JOHNNY exploded in a general burst of

fury, frustration, defeat, disappointment and debacle.

'ARRGHHHHHHHH!!!!!!!!!!!!!' he expressed.

'I'm an innocent man in a living hell and there's a father and son shagging in my cell.'

Smearing his own excrement over the four walls of the cell, he butted the table with his bare head and threw himself down into a thrashing mass of disgruntled humanity.
'I can't stand it, I can't stand it,' he screamed in an attempt to tell people that he couldn't stand it.

Running directly into the cell wall, he punched, kneed, kicked and spat at the bricks in general hopeless attack. The bricks kept on being in a way that is too deep for humans to understand. Whatever, the bricks stayed up and JOHNNY didn't.

Stunned, bleeding and coughing blood he spasmed onto the floor and convulsed into the bunk beds, banging his head so much it got him really mad. Then he collapsed in a pile of low self-esteem, hacking at his arms, grabbing his throat and squeezing his nuts into a fold of his guts. In a final and hopeless attempt to end it all he leapt on the table and jumped for the wall.

'Dense' Donny's ample rear-end loomed before him like a huge black hole and LITTLE JOHNNY hit it head first, taking a deflection and ending up with his head against a pipe. It was a windpipe.

'MMMMMMMMMmmmmm,' minced 'Dense' Donny. 'Now that's what I call a rear entry!'

Then a screw banged on the door.

'What's with the noise?' he enquired in an enquiring manner. 'Which of you apes are up to bum japes when there's blokes trying to get some kip?'

'Were not the ones you want,' winced Donny Sr. 'It ANUS, mate.'

BOOM BOOM!!!!!!!!

The doors were closing along the landing.

28 - SEX

Weak from watching a TWAT demolish a turd curry, VINCE needed something bad.

'What's up?' SHAZ shunted.

'I need something bad,' he grunted.

'I can be bad,' she punted, throwing back her head and ramming her fingers into her crotch. Ripping open her top, she allowed her bursting breasts to assault his midriff as she pumped manfully away below rubbing and grunting hard. Throwing herself wildly onto her back, she oozed pleasure as the passion in her heated loins built to bursting point. Throbbing mightily, she rolled onto her front, thrusting hard with her pelvis as her fingers probed her innermost spaces and smeared themselves slowly along the top of her glistening thighs. Leaking love juices in a squelchy spurt, she teased her throbbing loins into a blood reddened medley of slippery sexual tension.

She came with an explosion that sent her taught body into rhythmic gymnastics and she moaned long and loud into the fading waves of ecstasy.

'Bloody hell,' thought VINCE, 'If she acts like this at a crowded bus stop what's she gonna do when we got home?'

29 - FOOD

It was a hospital ward. He was a police inspector. His job was inspect. There was a doctor. His job was doctoring. The inspector as talking to him.

'We brought a bus load of old biddies and blokes in here,' he ened, opening a little, 'surely some of them must have seen some-ing. Are they all dead?'

'Hell no,' huffed the Doc. 'Comatose, not dead.'

'Have you noticed any evidence of life in their brains?'

'Get serious Inspector, they're pensioners.'

'Oh yeah, sorry. Will they ever show any sign of life?'

'Sure,' shuffled the Doc. 'Most of them are up and about.'

'Yer what? Then they must be okay?'

'Not at all. Think about it, most coppers can walk upright with eir eyes open for fifteen minutes at a time. It doesn't mean I'd find y evidence of brain activity if I examined them.'

'I guess you're right,' guessed the inspector.

Then the inspector slithered into the ward. Clocking a biddy with a buddy he blundered over and opened a little more. Hell, it felt good to get that fart out. Later he asked the biddy:

'Did you see STIG BIG, ELVIS TWAT and TYRONE HOOD LUM anywhere near that bus that got smashed?'

'Ooh yes, dear,' sighed one. 'All of the other pensioners were stunned but I clearly heard them coming on the scene and deciding to tip all the pensioners into the police station to frame them for killing the police.'

'Did you see anything else?' said the inspector, verging on a trouser-filler of an orgasm.

'Yes, I saw this UFO full of weird squid-like things skidding to stop down by the docks.'

Shit, this biddy was out to lunch. The Doc was right.

'Feeding time,' frittered a massive nurse slopping a massive steaming pan into a massive feeding trough. Out of the steaming vat fell gristle and fat, a few lumps that looked like dumps and all the rest of it that smelled like a cess pit. It lay in the trough festering. Then it stank, smelled rank and cooled in the tank to look like wank floating brown sauce . Soon it looked like the freshly oozing maggot-riddled insides of a week-dead hippie lying in the piss trench of the rock festival from Hell before transmogrifying itself to appear as the stinking diarrhoea of a thousand dead-cat eating tramps who had strained the last drop of watery dump out of stinging ring-pieces as they squatted over a blocked septic tank with the lid off. After that it just got too disgusting for words.

A ward full of pensioners plunged their faces into the slop and started slopping.

'Mmmm,' they hummed.
'A warm meal. We know when we're well off.'

Later one of them said to another: 'Do you know, most people can't spell DIARRHOEA?

'I thought he was the heavyweight champion of Wales,' said the other.

'Nah, slobbered the first one, 'that's Sugar Diabetes.'

30 - VIOLENCE

The bus ride home took forever. Everyone kept staring at SHAZ
and wondering if she'd do an encore. VINCE kept staring at his lap and
wondering if people could work out his pulse.

In through the door and she TASTED THE PASTE with
passion in an orgasmic frenzy that left him thrashing. Then he passed
out.

STIG BIG smashed the door to matchwood, casting a burly
shadow. In his wake came ELVIS TWAT and TYRONE HOODLUM.

'Turn us in for framing that Dad and his lad, would yer,' grunted the BIG lad. 'We'll learn yer.'

And they did.

Dragging a six foot razor blade behind them they tipped it up,
bunged VINCE on the top end and booted him along, forcing him to
use his bollocks as brakes. He felt the fine edge of the blade cutting
through his sack and slicing his bollocks in two. The sharp, searing
pain of his tearing testicles brought tears to his eyes. He spilled onto
the floor, roughly ripped and ragged. TYRONE did his maths home-
work, counting out loud as he broke ribs. It could've been worse, he'd
forgotten what came after seven.

VINCE came out of shock and felt pain beyond belief as STIG sank his cannibal gnashers into his knee cap and wrenched it off in a stinging swing of the head that left him looking at a hole that bled. Spitting out VINCE's knee cap, STIG slobbered blood into his eyes as ELVIS and TYRONE bent his arms backwards until his shoulders snapped. VINCE felt his bones resist before they started to splinter. Some general cracking was followed by clear snaps and a dull mulchy thud as each shoulder joint fell apart. He figured there were better ways to spend an afternoon. The pain choked him beyond screaming until ELVIS TWAT rodgered him with a fist and ripped him with a razor.

'AAAAWWWWW FUCKKK!!!!!!' VINCE rasped, reasonably, 'till he gargled blood in a coppery flood.

Scooping out VINCE'S insides, ELVIS TWAT skipped rope over a fresh intestine and then slipped on his liver.

'You've killed him too soon!' ranted STIG. 'If you keep 'em just barely alive, I can carve off fresh steaks for weeks.'

'Yeah,' tottered the TWAT, 'you might be short of a warm meal or two but all I've gotta do is slap a couple of straps on that gaping wound and I've made myself a well-hard RUCKSACK!!!!!!'

'Aahhhhh,' VINCE screamed, 'AAhhhhhh.'

'What's the score,' slobbered SHARON, waking him up.

He clocked her womanly curves and the phenomenal beauty of her firm legs.
'STIG, ELVIS and TYRONE to beat me by a knockout in the first round,' he fragged in total fear.

'You were just having a bad dream after passing out from the blow job of this or any century,' she dribbled accurately.
'I'll try and leave you conscious next time.'

He did get some sleep after that but - from then on - huge and mighty forms that do not live like living men moved slowly through the mind by day and were a trouble to his dreams.

31 - SEX

'I'll not put my fist up another bloke's bum for nowt,' argued LITTLE JOHNNY GOER, reasonably.

'Would you do it for a crisp fiver and twenty Bensons?' dithered Dense Donny Sr.

WHUMP!!!!!!!!!!

Whubble, whubble, whubble [Pant, pant, pant]

[FIST, FIST, FIST]

Aahhhhhh!!!!!!!

'There you go.'

'Cheers.'

'Don't smoke 'em all at once.'

Later, LITTLE JOHNNY savoured the rush of prime Benson smoke and pontificated about his predicament.

'I'm an innocent man in a living hell, and I've started fisting blokes whilst locked in my cell,' he roared with a mighty roar.

True enough, the twenty three hour lock-up had turned him a treat and the twenty three hours after that had led him to defeat. He quit fighting and joined them, Dense Donny and Dense Donny Sr that was. Anyway, once you've had your head up, accidental or not, anything else seems easy. Hell, the five minutes it had taken to ease his head out of Dense Donny's hole had their good side. At least - in the dense darkness inside Dense Donny - he didn't have to look at the slops bucket and general squalor. That really was disgusting.

In the corner Dense Donny Sr started a poster campaign. Above a drawing of a bending bloke and another guy grinning and holding a fiver and some fags he wrote: 'Don't be daft, work your shaft!!!!!'

The same picture was already on a few other posters that said:

'It's cute to sell your chute.'

'Earn some smokes for a poke.'

and

'Life is one huge biological accident. Anyone who thinks there is a point is mentally ill. All effort to improve on this hopeless position simply prolongs the agony. Cynical acts of prostitution make complete sense in this situation.'

'I'm not sure about the last one,' jabbered JOHNN. 'That'll give the real thickos a headache.'

'Yeah,' dinged Dense Donny Sr, 'but they'll be stood still so long trying to make sense of it that I'll have their trousis' down, myself up and the smokes in their hand before they've sussed anything.'

'That's mighty clever thinkin' for a 'Dense' guy,' jiffed LITTLE JOHNNY.

'Nah,' grunted Dense Donny Sr, 'I just remember my first time with a bloke. He asked me to read the back of a crisp packet. I must've been stood there for half an hour trying to figure out the ingredients. When me headache cleared I noticed my ring was stinging like it had been sandpapered.'

'Yuk!' yukked Johnny. 'How the hell did that get you into turning full-time?'

'It wuz prison done that,' grunted the older Dense one. 'There comes a time in every con's life when he sees he's got himself, four walls, some general squalor and his cell mate's bum. It ain't exactly romantic, Son, but it'll see you through a ten stretch.'

Later, JOHNNY roared poetically:

'This is an important moment in my story
I could get my freedom or turn all whorey
If I don't prove my innocence right away
I'll be out in ten years as a well rammed gay
Our SHARON's made an offer to that EAGER lad
She'll TASTE THE PASTE if he springs me and Dad
I hope for my sake EAGER's no quitter...

...'Cos it ain't like me to take it up the shitter........ I'm only a little guy and a ten stretch could leave me ripped and ragged.'

32 - FOOD

VINCE was EAGER for SHARON. He was also EAGER for food.

SHARON was EAGER for VINCE. She was also eager for food.

'I'm EAGER,' eased VINCE, honestly.

'Yeah, me too,' oozed SHARON, orgasmically.

'Food or a fuck?' he spouted, focusing the problem to a fine point.

'Dunno,' she dithered, 'let's toss for it.'

They did, VINCE came first with a mighty spurt that spurted mightily. SHARON was a close second with a gush and a rush and a hand in her bush.

Then they got sorted in the kitchen.

It might have been a cheap pizza but SHARON's way with a crisp lettuce gave it life and VINCE chopped, whapped and scooped in bacon bits, fresh peppers and the last of his sad hunk of Red Leicester cheese.

Twenty minutes of warm clinging wafts of smell from the oven left them demented with temptation and when the cheesy magnificence of the melted top emerged into the light of the kitchen they could hardly contain themselves. Smearing salad cream into the crisp lettuce SHARON dipped in a finger and licked the yellow cream that ran the length of her hand.

'MMMMM,' she dribbled, 'I could get used to TASTING THE PASTE.'

Insane with hunger, fear and raging desire for the fearsome firmness that heaved out of her low cut top, VINCE EAGERly fed his desire with the first slice of pizza. The warm dough sent a soft cloud of heat into his mouth, through the walls into the top of his head and bound several miles of blood vessels into his every fibre. The under stated confidence of the consistent mozzarella cheese eased its way to VINCE's taste buds where it lounged around long enough kick in some life. The pepperoni had a beefy firmness pushed forward by spicy pepper. The light grease that worked its way out of the tiny slices slung around long enough to do the job and vanished before it set congealing lumps to work making SHARON and VINCE feel guilty.

Solidly, magnificently, with the kind of confidence that comes from not having to try too hard, the pizza did the job. It was honest, it was dependable, its knew it's business and it shuffled down their gullets in slowly sliding warm lumps of heated satisfaction.

Later, they finished off with the firm crispness of a well tossed and slightly pasted salad. It's light, cool fresh assurance woke up their minds.

'We watched that TWAT demolish a turd curry and walk away with little more than a bad attitude and a seething stomach,' opened VINCE, with a woken up mind. 'He's as hard as a bloke that's hard,' he added, obviously. 'I'd love your luscious lips on my love pump for life. But, it strikes me that any attempt to get a life-time's head, is only gonna result in me being dead.'

'I'm starting to have feelings for you,' she oozed, starting to feel him. 'I'd hate to be left with your corpse, a jar of KY and my right hand,' she added, honestly.

'ELVIS TWAT, is a twat even when he's poisoned, everyone knows TYRONE HOODLUM's old man is the law around here and STIG BIG is thick, violent and prone to bouts of instant cannibalism on a good day. The only advantage I've got over those three brainless gits is that I've got a brain,' volunteered VINCE. 'I'll have to think up the kind of cunning plan that helps pathetic wimps in stories about pathetic wimps taking on HARD BASTARDS. The kind of cunning plan that convinces everyone following the story that they too could be a hero.'

[AT THIS POINT THE MUSIC ROSE SLOWLY BEHIND HIM AND HIS VOICE GOT FIRMER THAN YER AVERAGE WIMPY HERO'S KIND OF VOICE. EVERYONE ON THE ENTIRE PLANET GOT A CLOSE UP OF HIS FACE AND HIS JAW WAS LOOKING FIRM, AND HEROIC. HE HADN'T GROWN ANY MORE MUSCLES THOUGH.]

'I've got a brain,' roared VINCE. 'And I'll use it to take on those thick psychos and force them into confessing what they did to MR GOER and LITTLE JOHNNY.'

[THE MUSIC GOT REALLY LOUD, SHARON STARTED TO DRIBBLE A LOT. HER MOUTH GOT A BIT DAMP TOO.]

'Go for it VINCE,' she fragged. 'Say something deep and heroic.'

Screaming to be heard over the music, VINCE went for it.

'I'm smarter than them and I'll fight with every ounce of the intelligence what I've got, know what I mean, SHARRY?' he howled, heroically. 'For without brains what is a man but a device for turning sweet smelling food into foul smelling shit????????'

Without her hands coming within six inches of her gusset,

SHARON came on the spot. Then she threw herself backwards over the sofa and came some more. Later, she fell face down on the carpet coming all the time and then she came as she thought about how much she'd just come.

'OOOhhhhhh, VINCE,' she drooled damply. 'Keep talking like that and I can keep using my right hand for cooking.'

33 - VIOLENCE

Shit, piss, fuck cunt. Well that was ELVIS TWAT's idea of a good night. A decent scrap or ten to round things off with the added bonus of some head breaking, arm wrenching and grinding noses into his knee cap was a bonus. But, hell, you can't have everything and this night he was getting NOWT!!!!

'You can't have everything and this night I've had NOWT!!!!' he roared with a mighty roar. He'd staggered and retched his way into his street, guts seething, gums bleeding with an expression like a baby teething. That wasn't the only thing he was doing like a baby and the seeping sludge was starting to budge in his pants.

Did ELVIS TWAT love violence or WHAT???!!!

Well he did, until now. The violence that was - literally -
beating the shit out of his guts was driving him nuts. Psychotic microbes with microbe Doc Martens complete with spiked steel toe-caps were searching out nerve ends and spiking them with mighty
spiking kicks. An army of wire wool Weetabix were roaming his insides to put him in a fix. The breakfast cereal from Hell was making ELVIS yell. They turned blow torches on his pancreas just to be cantankerous. Gas and heaving sludge made his insides budge. The torturing tide of turd could easily be heard.

'SLUBBB, QUWU, SLEERKK, WUBBLLLLLE,' it oozed as it festered along.

ELVIS could hear it. 'Shit,' he shuffled with biological accuracy.
olence from the outside he could TWAT to defeat, but this seething
idge attack had got big ELVIS beat.

Ragged blasts of ring-stinging thunder were tearing his jeans
d the briefs that were under his jeans.

F-f-f-f-f-A-A-A-ARRRRTTTTTT!!!!!!

'Arghh!' screamed ELVIS. 'That measured on the Richter scale
d dislodged me pelvis.'

It did.

Shoulder charging a lamp-post, ELVIS TWAT winced as his
lvic girdle righted itself and left a dent in the council's finest concrete
nstruction.

The TWAT considered his position and considered himself to
about three feet from the lamp post, two hundred yards from his
use and thirty seconds away from a colon emptying that would fill
s jeans to bursting and send stinking sludge into the street. Fuck
iew, he was no stranger to strong curry but this shit bag of a shaft
aker had set his mighty guts on a real earthquaker.

His thirty seconds had run out along with the seam on the arse
his jeans.

F-f-f-f-f-F-F-A-A-AAAAAARRRRTTTT!!!!!!!!

'Arghhh, my arse.'

PHUT-PHUT-PHUT-SPLLLTTTTTT!!!

It was the "SPLLLTTTTT!!!" that hurt his pride beyond all
easure and released cold shivers to roam his body at leisure.

'Ooh, fuck.'

Stinking and steaming the brown tide hit the street. The colou
in the double yellow lines started to run and a rat in a local sewer ran
his lawyer. 'AARgghhhhhh,' with a blistering butt and a heaving gut t
mighty TWAT heaved himself round to view the splat. There were
yellow streaks in the foul smelling tide that had hit the street
two yards wide.

'Mummy!'

He'd wanted women many times but now the only one who
would do....and her washing machine, were two hundred yards down
the road. That two hundred yards looked like.....well, a bloody long
way.

Just then, a UFO full of green-eyed squid creatures skidded to
halt some distance away. It would have skidded to halt closer but it
slipped on a fetid tide of foul smelling shit and rode the spewmongou
surf into a car park.

'Consider relativity,' mumbled the green-eyed leader lining his
troops up against an aging Volkswagon with no hub caps. 'We green-
eyed squid creatures may traverse galaxies and that but our
understanding of relativity has knackered us in our mission to tangle
with that fit and wholesome sweetheart of the allied forces in World
War Two, Vera Lynn.'
He stopped for a second.
'Relativity has something to do with the way things relate to
each other,' he added obviously.

The way ELVIS related to his Mum would be sorely tested whe
he presented his jeans for a combined attack by her and Square Deal
Surf. Right now he was surfing a second wave of sludge slopping
against his sphincter.

'Relativity,' added the captain, 'is about the way things relate,
the perception of that relationship and the deep, eternal forces which
control all things that are and will be.'

The deep eternal forces of ELVIS TWAT's digestion were about to bring another tidal wave of total turd terror tumbling onto several yards of unsuspecting pavement. 'ARGHHH!!!!!!,' arghhhed ELVIS, clutching his stomach, buttocks and a lamp-post.

'Cut the complicated crap and give us an example,' spouted a squid to his captain.

'That crap would dissolve Technetium, cutting it would be impossible,' grunted the captain, eyeing the stinking sludge that continued to budge. 'It's crisping that bloke's anus in a way that is quite heinous. But his situation that's so demanding gives us an understanding, of relativity, well the start of one anyway.'

'Giz it,' grunted a squid, so the Captain did.

'Consider that sad and seething Fuck whose arse is oozing muck. You see, when a bloke is feeling fine two hundred yards takes no time. When a bloke's arse is spewing volcanic crap in a series of trouser flapping eruptions interspersed with deep pungent farts that would have a ward of hopeless specimens on life support machines upping sticks and running full pelt for the fall-out shelter, and when at the same time, his hard man status is in serious doubt because a violent assault on his physical well being by a total turd Vindaloo is working it's way through, and when the long yellow burn streaks are smeared on his bum cheeks, and when the whole fucking street is sensing his defeat, you see, fellow green-eyed squid creatures, in those circumstances the same two hundred yards can seem like a mile. That's relativity.'

The captain was right but he was standing in shite. 'Here comes the fetid tide, we should all hop inside,' he finished.

They did.

ELVIS stumbled on, trying to nurse his suffering, swearing and muttering.

'SHIT, PISS, FUCK, CUNT!!!!!'

That was ELVIS TWAT's idea of a good night, but right now the only idea he had was something about stumbling another two hundred yards and getting home alive.

34 - SEX

Strimming strimmers sent strimmer sounds all around. The
cops were hard at work in the TWAT's garden. ELVIS' step-dad had a
hard on. 'This is a hard on,' he howled howlingly, pointing with his
finger and his hard on. 'Soon it will be a hard in,'

NAT TWAT - mother of ELVIS TWAT - considered that, then
she got damp, got down, came seven times with a mighty moan and
once quietly on her own. The last one was long and selfish, she lay on
her back and smelled like a shell fish. She'd used her hand to bring an
eighth spasm when her knackered husband had withdrawn from her
spasm. His hard on and hard in had turned to a soft on and flop out.

'What's with them strimmers and cops in the garden?' she
pushed.

'They're doing us lawn again,' he hummed, selecting the shirt
with the least dirt.

'What did you tell 'em this time,' she fragged, fumbling for a
fag.

'The usual - anonymous tip off about a body in a shallow
grave.'

It was true, PAT DOZY-TWAT - double barrelled, beer bel-
lied, lotsa quarrels, fuckin' smelly stepfather of ELVIS TWAT - had a
decent line in tipping off the cops about evidence in his garden. It was
bollocks but it got 'em out mob handed with strimmers and they even
tipped the borders down a treat - not to mention taking the cuttings

away for forensic.....well whatever they do that is forensic. The DOZY-TWAT hadn't cut his own lawn in two years.

'I'm not such a DOZY-TWAT when you think about how clever I am,' he grinned.

Then again, the cops had been a bit slow to respond this time. All available man-power had been diverted to stopping, stripping and searching every fit looking lass in town following an anonymous tip off that there was a stunning piece of skirt bent on a suicide bombing hiding explosives close to her skin. The overtime claim on this one was breaking all records but still the red-eyed dribbling coppers forced themselves on. 'Keep it up lads,' urged the Chief Constable to one shift who couldn't even keep their tongues up any-more. When they ogled the town without finishing the job, they called the lasses back in one big mob. They made them search each other and caused some offence when the official police photographer came on his lens, which gutted him something serious. 'I'm gutted something serious,' he growled. 'I could have made a load with that one shot and instead I've shot my load and knackered the lot.'

There was a rumour that the tip off about the fit lass was a wind up by somebody on the inside who just wanted an easy life and an effortless feeling of satisfaction. What confused everybody was the cunning behind it. Where would the police have got the idea about using an anonymous tip off for their own ends? Which, incidentally, were looking a bit frayed after hours spent throbbing hard and steady against rough police trousers.

Anyway, the weary mob now had another job, strimming and trimming the TWAT's lawn.

'Smells like shit in here,' coughed a copper, smelling shit.

'Oh Shit!!!' shuffled another.

'What's with that shit?' shimmied a third.

What was causing all the fuss was the strong smell of turd. And it was getting stronger, and stronger.

'ARGHHHH!!!!!!!' arghhed ELVIS TWAT, argghhing his way into his house and facing the local constabulary. Trailing two hundred yards of steaming skidmarks, a ton of flies dying from indigestion and the lawyer for a sewer rat with standards to keep up, ELVIS TWAT kept nothing up and gushed his last blast in a furious ring ripping fart that almost stopped his heart. He fell where he stopped, soaking in his slops.

'He's wanted for doing pensioners and police,' retched a rozzer.

'I don't want him for fuckin' nowt,' stated a second, honestly.

They took in the unconscious form of ELVIS TWAT as NAT TWAT and PAT DOZY-TWAT slid down the stairs.

'That's our ELVIS, ripped, ragged and oozing stinking shits with his trousers ripped to bits,' said the woman who had brought him into this world several years before and brought herself with her hand within the last few minutes. She thought about the deep affection she felt for her poor, suffering son. Then she thought about her carpets.

'Get that stinking shit heap out of here,' she coo-ed with motherly affection.

35 - FOOD

'So, does everyone in here go in for bum japers, scrotum capers, and the company of mutual masturbators?' opened Mr GOER.

'Don't open in here Dad,' said LITTLE JOHNNY GOER, 'Unless you're after crisp notes, fresh smokes and random rear entry pokes.'

LITTLE JOHNNY GOER might have turned a treat, driven to distraction by a long lock up and the breaking in monotony offered by a throbbing cock up. His Dad was still straight. But then the old git never did have much ambition. 'You never did have much ambition you old git,' said LITTLE JOHNNY GOER.

'I'd call it pacing meself, son.' countered the old git with no ambition. 'I'll grant you the crisp cash and tobacco stash that comes from your regular rectal bash. But you've got me wrong, I've scored big time. Check it out:'

LITTLE JOHNNY did. A crowd was gathering in the education wing, a little stove was roaring and Mr GOER was doing a fine trade in stuffed Woodpecker. All around, cons slobbered sauces and spat small bones as a bloke from the telly spoke in cultured tones.

'Consider the Woodpecker,' said the telly bloke.

Several dozen hardened criminals were already considering it the finest slice of meat they had tasted since they tongued those closest to them before they had been taken far away from those closest to them, sort of thing. Sizzling on a sparse looking spit next to a supposedly ambitionless git were the scrawny looking remains of an endangered species. Hot and meaty, with a lingering insistent flavour supported by a stuffing of dry roasted nuts and gravy soaked bread-crumbs, the Woodpeckers were driving the captives crazy with every crunch.

'You don't get much meat on a Woodpecker, but by the time you've shifted twenty the warm satisfaction is starting to spread from your toes to your head,' a prisoner pontificated.

'It's stronger than chicken, weaker than duck - Woodpecker's that taste that makes prisoners shout....fuck!'

'FUCKKK!!!!!!!!!!!!!,' roared the prisoners.

'Shut the fuck up!' talked the telly presenter who was doing a presentation on stage.

Sir David Attenbum was famous for wildlife shows and MR GOER's bird-watching background had pulled off the surprise coup of con's social calender when the telly star - hoping his good works would earn him a peerage - had agreed to talk nature to those of a criminal nature. He'd come armed with a truck load of Woodpeckers and a few crates of barbecue sauce. Mr GOER was cooking the pile as Sir David Attenbum turned on the style. The audience was munching like mad. The clincher in pulling the big crowd had been the billing. The talk was on 'Saving boxing and stopping boring bastards from trying to ban it.'

The telly talker talked: 'My knowledge of animals tells me that Woodpeckers have a sponge like substance on the front of their brains to protect them from injury as they headbutt trees. We can remove this and pump it into boxers' heads. I estimate that it will take the sponges from around fifty Woodpeckers to protect one boxer.'

'YAY!' roared the mob. 'Crunchy chunks all round in abundance.'

The telly man ripped the head off another bird, lopped in a long thing and pulled out a sponge, of sorts. 'I'll admit it doesn't look like much but pumped into the head of a fighting man it has properties that will protect his.....

'Oi,' interrupted the one in the mob with GCSE English and a chunk of the riverbank's finest in his gob. 'Isn't anyone bothered about slaughtering endangered birds to protect a bunch of thugs who would probably be in prison if they weren't out there endangering their long-term health for the short term gain of a bunch of money grabbing managers and the like? I mean Woodpeckers are wholesome and nice, unlike boxing managers.'

'That may be true,' narrated the famous naturalist, 'but I've done one programme on Woodpeckers so I can't see the chance of getting another one soon. I say 'Sod the Woodpeckers,' there's no more money for me in those long beaked bastards unless I can corner the market in brain-protection for boxers.'

'YAY,' roared the mob, 'Crunchy goodness and barbecue sauce, is nearly as good as sexual intercourse.'

In the corner, LITTLE JOHNNY GOER slipped his hand slowly into the steamy mitt of 'the boy from Paris with the tasty piece of Aris' AKA currency smuggler, FRENCH FRANK. The French bloke liked a strong smoke, as many French blokes do. Despite the odd packet of continental lung-busting baccy, FRENCH FRANK had shuffled through prison with a face like a bludgeoned bulldog.
    'Don't look like yer survivin' your time too well,' said a prisoner, looking serious one day.
    'Yeah,' mumbled FRENCH FRANK, 'each day I think only of my bollocks and how to use them.'

The arrival of tasty LITTLE JOHNNY GOER and his turning during the long lock up of the short night/day had changed FRENCH FRANK's facial expression. Now he looked like a bulldog that hadn't been bludgeoned. The boy looked at JOHNNY, JOHNNY looked at the boy. The two entwined and, since love is blind, they didn't see the chaos going on behind.

The stimulating spices of the sauce bought at cut prices led the convicted mob to act on their own devices.

'One, two, three, four. That talk was okay but we want more.' roared the mob, stamping their prison boots. The telly talker had presented a corker but the mob was swaying, for action they were baying.'

'BAY!!!!!!!!!!!!!!!!!!!!' bayed the bunch. 'We want action!'

'That crunchy lunch didn't satisfy this bunch, they need something which punch, or they'll give yer bollocks a scrunch.' said a prisoner to Mr GOER.

'Don't worry, lad, I've got it covered,' grunted Mr GOER. 'Bring on the Albanians.'

An Albanian folk band had been banged up for a week in the jail. They kept themselves to themselves, until, that is, they were brought on-stage by Mr GOER, after which they brought themselves, by hand, by mouth and in full view of an ecstatic crowd, all to the sound of a few sad looking drums and something that looked like a guitar and sounded like shit. By the time the last Albanian was pulled off in public, Mr GOER had pulled off a show to remember.

Later, in his cell, Mr GOER turned to face his cell mate and came clean: 'Cos people figure I'm an old git with no ambition I've got a job in the prison offices doing some filing,' he said. 'I saw the paperwork on them Albanians. They're a folk band that got lottery money to do some cultural exchange visit. They were supposed to play a few dates up and down the country but they only lasted one night before they got arrested in their hotel. They came down for breakfast and clocked the meat mountain keeping warm in the big serving tins. When they read a sign saying "Help yourself" it was more than these underpaid buggers could handle. They went into a traditional Albanian folk dance that involved dropping their trousers, grunting like good uns and shooting their collective loads. To Albanian peasants it represents responding to days of plenty by ceremonially spilling their seed. To the owners of a three star hotel with ambitions to hold conferences it represented half an hour of a chambermaid's time, a bucket of top grade carpet shampoo and the kind of write up in the local paper that costs business. Personally speaking I've got some sympathy for those Albanian lads. They are as poor as fuck and it was a serious pile of bacon.'

'So you organised an encore to make your fellow prisoners roar,' rasped his cell mate.

'Yeah,' grunted Mr GOER, 'I knew the sight of sizzling Woodpeckers would arouse the Albanians. People reckon I'm an old git with no ambition but I've made a shit load on that show and I've got a waiting list weeks ahead for Woodpecker sarnies. Prison has turned our Johnny to mincing, preening and pathetic queening. He's taking french letters from FRENCH FRANK, a greasy sod with hot money in the bank. But prison is turning me too. I've let my standards slip and I'm losing my grip. I'm wheeling and dealing without any feeling. I'll sell my fellow man for anything I can, I'll endanger a Woodpecker's ass for a handful of brass. I'm on the slippery slope that ends in lack of hope.'

'S'funny,' said his cell mate, 'I thought you were an old git with no ambition.'

36 - VIOLENCE

Things had moved on a bit in the police station. 'Things are moving on a bit, eh, Sarge?' splurted a plod, obviously.

'You could say that,' slobbered the Sarge.

'I just did,' splurted the first plod.

The plod was right, this guy could almost string a sentence together, the Sarge scribbled his name down for promotion.

Things moving on included the moving out of Cressida Pemberton Slag and her meaty carcass. Tyrone's turd in the handbag torture had done for her sanity what that atom bomb on Hiroshima did for the hanging baskets of that city.
'Get that woman out of here,' sobbed the sarge, stabbing a finger at the whimpering mass of blubber, blubber, breasts and more blubber that was Cressida. 'She stinks of shit.'

'It ain't her stinks of shit,' spouted the plod, 'It's that mighty TWAT on his way in here.'

He was right.

Grappling with a gross of constabulary and stinking up a storm, the unmistakable bulk of ELVIS TWAT was being man-hauled, keel-hauled, road-hauled and black-balled across the plod panda park. The black mass beating ELVIS' ass were surrounded by a black cloud that were buzzing and loud.

'Must be a million flies chasing that shitty smell from big EL,' pontificated a plod, poetically.

And there were.

The shitty smell stank to hell as ELVIS was pushed into the cell. TYRONE HOODLUM clocked the approaching shit storm and retched in the corner.

'AARGHHHHH!!!!!!' he argghued reasonably, clocking the instant justice of the way the plods had - in a round about fashion - now dumped a turd in his handbag. 'You fucking plods have clearly beaten the shit out of my mate and I can see the seventh shade seeping through the ripped remains of his jeans.'

'Urghh,' slobbered the stinking spewing specimen that was the once mighty ELVIS TWAT. 'It was them bastards in the Bulimic Bengali that fed me a curry that left me sprawling,' opened ELVIS TWAT.

'He's opening, run for it!' rasped a rozzer running.

ELVIS TWAT opened, exploded and sent a turd tidal wave wafting under the door. A gross of coppers saw it seeping and decided it was gross.

'Hey!' yelled TYRONE HOODLUM, hammering the door like hell. 'I've got a buddy with a problem, problem, buddy with a problem.'

A passing plod raised his bonce to the cell bars, clocked the expiring ELVIS TWAT and said, sympathetically, 'You're a stretcher case, baby.'

And he was.

He was stretched on the cell floor and his stupendous stink was stretching stomachs something serious and driving hardened plods delirious.

'OOhhh fuck,' fragged TYRONE HOODLUM, what's the score with this?'

'Psycho 1, Plod 2,' butted in the Old Bill together.

And it was.

Just then TYRONE HOODLUM collapsed in a hopeless heap feeling cheap. Two thirds of the RAIDERS OF THE LOW FOREHEAD were banged up in steaming stench in a cell with only one bench. They might have done for the pensioners and battered a pile of plods but now things were looking grimmer than a baby playing with a strimmer. If they were gonna break out and get even it was gonna take a fight, or ten.

Then the flies arrived. A streaming tide three feet wide passed the cell and headed inside. Heading for the steaming shite they terrorised the RAIDERS into the night. Rediscovering their fearsome might, TYRONE and ELVIS put up a fight.

TYRONE swatted handfuls of the buzzing bastards. Crunching out their tiny lives with the frustration of years of being crushed under the unrelenting jackboot of his father - SIR CLEMENT HOODLUM. 'You'll never amount to anything you stinking pile of unspeakable filth,' he yelled at the recently crushed remains of a sizeable bluebottle. The bluebottle oozed a small stream of stinking, unspeakable filth, slipped off the wall, fell into the shit and never amounted to anything.

ELVIS' weakened frame rediscovered it's sadistic touch in the face of an attack by creatures infinitely weaker. Swatting with both hands, his head and one kneecap he crushed insect exoskeletons by the gross, plastering the cell wall with oozing brown insect blood and leaving black trail marks down the white cell brick. For one second he glimpsed a row of fatally wounded flies twitching their legs to a solid hip-hop beat, except that there was no music and the tiny bastards would have been two thick to understand it if there was. Later, he grabbed at a big black bastard of a buzzer, stuck it between his thumb and forefinger and squeezed it till its eyes popped out and almost hit his. 'What you looking at?' he howled hilariously. Dimly ELVIS though there was nothing like simple slaughter to restore a man's sapped strength. Hanging onto this thought he turned on three stray wasps in the corner, hit them with a sharp smelling blast of bum gas and sent them to the great honey pot in the sky.

'Oi, ELVIS!' hoodlummed TYRONE. 'Do you think there's an afterlife?'

'Dunno, TYRONE,' twatted ELVIS, 'but mess wi me and you'll soon find out.'

Having killed almost every six legged life form with wings in the surrounding area, ELVIS TWAT AND TYRONE HOODLUM collapsed on the apology for a bench that had managed to escape the seeping slop. Slowly one shit-caked fly slipped out of the slime and eased itself onto the bench. The two RAIDERS looked. ELVIS dived, pinning the little fucker by its legs and TYRONE took to torturing wit the tastefulness only true blue bloods can muster. 'What's the square root of sixteen?' he howled.

The fly moved its five unpinned legs.

'Wrong,' warned ELVIS.

The fly still moved all five legs.

RIP!!!!!!!

'Oi, you four legged freak, what's ten take away seven?'

The fly moved all four of it's legs. Etc etc.

Later it provided ELVIS and TYRONE with a good five minute of amusement as it walked circles around three of its severed legs. Late

LVIS won a bet when the one legged fly managed to move an inch between two notches in the bench.

'Are we a pair of cruel bastards who like nothing better than torture or destruction?' asked ELVIS.

'Dunno about that,' grunted TYRONE, 'I reckon we have our reasonable moments. C'mon for fuck's sake, the square root of sixteen easy.'

37 - SEX

STIG BIG surveyed the talent. Then he got to thinking. He thought it was only people who lived in towns that could think that every sheep was ugly. Out here, with a warm breeze, a setting sun and some fresh turnips to get them excited, some of this woolly jailbait could give a man more come on than he could handle. STIG was handling it manfully but with so much tottie in plain view he figured he'd finish the job in a sheep.

STIG BIG didn't know much, but he knew that people who lived in towns figured sheep fanciers stuck the back legs of the animals down their wellies to have their wicked way. STIG surveyed his solid leather boots and thought grandmaster sheep shagging. Wellies were pathetic next to the edge of a cliff. Within twenty minutes STIG, a fit looking young Herdwick and the last rays of the setting sun were making beautiful music on the edge of a quarry. Throbbing up a treat STIG stug forward and made his lover bleat. She wasn't up for it then but STIG's need was serious. His ruddy face ruddied as his strapping arms strapped and his racing blood raced. Soon his racing blood was racing as his ruddy face was ruddying and his strapping arms were strapping. Then his strapping arms strapped ....anyway, he was really going for it. The sheep was playing hard to get.

She 'BAA-ed,' and bleated, leaving STIG defeated.

'C'mon you ungrateful little bitch,' he grunted reasonably.

Grabbing her soft young fleece STIG felt enough lust to drive his testicles to a Richter scale registering detonation. Practically passing out, STIG gave a shout, 'URGHHHHH! C'mon you'se gonna love it.'

Throwing the sheep's head over the edge of the quarry, STIG got a result. Clocking the sheer drop, even the stubborn sheep figured that a swift splattering from the rear was better than a messy splattering on the rocks below. Swiftly the sheep pushed back as STIG hung on tight, stood his ground and lost a mugful in a millisecond.

'OOOOOOO-EEEEE-ARGHHHHHHHH,UNGHHHHHH, my pretty darlin!' he stigged impressively. He fell like a tree trunk landed in a pile of sheep shit and thought about the greatest sexual experience of his life. She bolted, bleated, took in the sunset and came back to lick his hand.

STIG surveyed her deep brown eyes and felt something deep inside him move more than he'd ever believed possible. He felt love, commitment and a meeting of souls. The future stopped looking like some vague plans for cleaning tractors, shovelling shit, shifting pints and breaking heads and started looking like...A Future. Deep in the slowly grinding cogs of his stunted apology for a brain he struggled to put his new view of the world into words. He sighed deeply, looked into the sunset, looked into her eyes and felt the satisfaction of a well drained scrotum. 'OOOOhhhhhh,' he sighed, 'fuckin' magic.'

38 - FOOD

If they'd been prisoners in a war the Geneva Convention would have sorted them for clothes and food. They were in a police cell so it didn't. After the night of the long fly massacre ELVIS TWAT and TYRONE HOODLUM kipped, stank and woke up well pissed off.

Two passing plods had a chat outside the cell.

'Why do people call us the pigs?' asked a raw recruit, being cute.

'Cos they don't know what bastards we really are,' answered an old hand, sounding bland.

'I know, and if I don't get some decent treatment soon I'll be blagging to my father - SIR CLEMENT HOODLUM. It may be Psych 1 Plod 2 but I know my rights.' shouted TYRONE HOODLUM. In truth, he knew a bit more than fuck all but a lot less than his rights. Then again, if your old man is the law you can get away with knowing nowt.

TYRONE had tried his hand at knowing something. The magazine publishing division of HOODLUM INDUSTRIES published part works and TYRONE had lasted a day in that. He'd gone in full of hope and left looking a dope. The part-work monthly encyclopedias were the backbone of HOODLUM PART-WORK ENCYCLOPEDIAS

TYRONE had been invited to a board meeting to add new titles to the list. He'd suggested 'The Wonderful World of Big Colour Pictures' an idea so stunning in it's cack brained simplicity that it got considered for a full twenty seconds. 'Just get a load of big colour pictures and bung them out every month,' TYRONE had talked.

'It's a bit too honest if you ask me, son,' said the Editor. 'It may be true that the public will buy any old shit so long as it's put over in big colour pictures but if we make it that obvious they'll turn on us.'

'I'll rip 'em apart if they do,' grunted TYRONE, honestly. 'Speaking of which I've got some pictures.' TYRONE tabled some severed ears, a kneecap sticking through the skin and bloke fumbling on a floor looking for the broken ends of his teeth. Luckily he tabled them as Polaroids. 'How about 'The Wonderful World of Kicking In Heads?' he asked hopefully.

'Not a hope,' grunted the Ed.

That was the way it went for half an hour until everyone turned and told TYRONE to fuck off, so he did. TYRONE would have torn the whole poncey lot of them in half with his bare hands, booted their entrails into a bucket for the pigs and fed their meat to his mate STIG but they worked for his Dad and that would have pissed off SIR CLEMENT something serious because replacing the whole lot would have involved the old bastard doing some proper work for a change.

Later he thought and thought and thought some more about the things that had been said. He sent in his final winning idea in a folder. 'My Life In Pictures' was tabled and tossed aside in seconds. It sounded great until somebody opened it and realised it contained a Polaroid of every turd TYRONE had had for two months. This confused TYRONE to a serious headache. 'S'funny' he sagged, slopping beer with STIG and ELVIS one night, 'The boss said the public would buy any old shit so long as it was put over in big colour pictures.'

'Life's shit,' grunted ELVIS, honestly.

'Eh?' said TYRONE.

'Life's shit,' said ELVIS again.

TYRONE clicked to the present and clocked the stinking mess. 'You know what?' grunted TYRONE. 'I remember you saying that once when I had my pile of Polaroid turds thrown back in my face by those ponces in the part-work bit of Dad's empire.' Coming to his senses TYRONE realised that life was shit. It was shit when they told him his ideas were crap and it was still shit now when there was him, ELVIS and four crap stained walls surrounding a floor full of shit.

'Let us out you fucking plod bastards or you'll answer to my Dad,' howled TYRONE.

They did, then they hosed them, dosed them - against the kind of germs that breed in shit - and sat them down for bacon and eggs and grilled them for a bit. 'Do you know owt about a load of dead plods and pummelled pensioners?' asked an inspector.

TYRONE and ELVIS admired their new clean clothes and knew that the plods were worried about coming clean to SIR CLEMENT about the way the two RAIDERS OF THE LOW FOREHEAD had been brow-beaten a bit and left to fester in shit.
    'Je ne regret nowt,' eased ELVIS.

Later TYRONE demanded to see his Dad's lawyer who told him to say nowt so he didn't. TYRONE and ELVIS caught a flash of the Mars bar in the lawyer's pocket and attacked it without mercy. Ripping the chunky bastard in half they savoured the strong sleek caramel, the wonderfully whipped cream interior and the light chocolate covering that shattered in their mouths, ran all over their tongues and woke up their taste buds for the length and strength of the mighty bar. ELVIS groaned as the caramel stuck to his front teeth and felt his starving brain go dizzy with delight as his tongue slopped sweetness from his incisors and rubbed it against the roof of his mouth. He considered storing slivers of caramel in the valleys of his top teeth but his need was serious. He sucked in his cheeks, felt the lingering lumps lumbering to his throat and swallowed them in one long lasting stream. Each solid mouthful of the monster chocolate snack brought new strength and hope. It was a king sized bar and the lawyer had a king sized hump on at losing it but he knew better than to tangle with the demented offspring of SIR CLEMENT HOODLUM.

'It's long, it's strong and it'll last you all day long,' grunted the lawyer.

'Humph' humphed ELVIS, 'Mars push the envelope on strength and taste, they make other chocolate treats look a waste.'

'Yeah,' grunted TYRONE, 'The wrappers black, the writing's red, and when you've finished you feel well fed.'

A watching plod noted it down and wondered if it might be used in evidence.

Then ELVIS too figured saying nowt was smart, so he sat there and thought about the shit curry that had weakened him to the point where he'd thought his life was over. Then he thought about the way that life was shit anyway so it figured that having the screaming shits was a way out of it. He figured that somewhere in this deep cess pit of swimming shit there was some meaning and if he could only figure it out then he could let people know something important and get famous or something. Then maybe life wouldn't be shit. Then again he couldn't figure any of this shit out for himself so how could he make other people understand?

Then he felt like having a shit, so he did. Surveying his first floating log in over a day, he looked hard at the strangely solid object. This was a shit and a half and in that moment he knew. He knew, in the shape of the shit, that he had it. Those tortured coils, the weaving that went nowhere and the way that the whole thing came to a pointless dead-end said it all. This shit floating before him represented all human life - ever. He looked, he wiped up, threw the papers on the floor and set off to phone an art gallery or something.

A plod caught sight of him shuffling out of the bog and ELVIS realised he'd have to be quick cos he was saying nothing, the way TYRONE's lawyer had said he should. It was funny that, cos since the lawyer had told them to say nowt ELVIS and TYRONE hadn't been able to speak so they couldn't ask him why they should say nowt.

Clocking the smell and remembering the hell of ELVIS and TYRONE's smelly cell the plod ran in and pulled the flush.

ELVIS looked, and seethed and gnashed his teeth as he realised that the Plod had sent his masterpiece round the U-bend. Then he collapsed in general pointlessness, hopelessness, lack of direction and bad attitude. The cop had flushed his future, his focus and all hope of fame. He knew in that moment that his life was down the bog, for ever.

Then again, life was shit like that.

39 - VIOLENCE

ELVIS TWAT and TYRONE HOODLUM looked grim at the copper.

The copper looked grim at ELVIS TWAT and TYRONE HOODLUM. The lawyer looked at the lot of them and figured that things looked grim. 'Things are looking grim for you lads,' grunted the copper. 'You may be saying nowt but there's evidence and witnesses, and a pile of dead police. You could confess now and save yourselves a grilling worse than what the bacon in your sarnies got. When we get to asking questions we go in hard and that ain't no place for pussies. We quizzed a gang about some thieving last week. One lad cried all the water out of his body, just imagine how his mother felt.'

ELVIS TWAT and TYRONE HOODLUM looked grim at the copper. The copper looked grim at ELVIS TWAT and TYRONE HOODLUM. The lawyer looked at the lot of them and asked if he could have a moment alone with his clients. He got it.

'It's looking grim,' grunted the lawyer when they were alone. 'SIR CLEMENT might be the law but the coppers emotions are raw. There are witnesses, bodies and a bent bus being investigated. Them witnesses may be pensioners but the plods might cook a statement that's as bent as like what the bus is bent, like, and then you two will be on your bike, to jail. It'll be all I can do to get you two out of this alive. Anyway, that handwriting on the note is a bit familiar and there's a burger van man who puts you on the scene at the time.'

If he put us there it must be his fault,' tried TYRONE hopelessly.

'That's hopeless,' grunted the lawyer. 'It'll take a miracle to get you out of this.'

TYRONE thought, then he thought some more, by the time he thought again he was really thinking. 'I think I've got it,' he grunted. Five minutes later he had a piece of paper and five minutes after that, with lots of sticking his tongue out, grunting and moving a pencil about he really had it. 'Deliver this and stand back,' he commanded handing the lawyer a note. The lawyer did.

STIG was surveying the sheep shed when the lawyer arrived. Taking in the talent, his trousers were taking the strain of a serious hard-on. His little darling was seriously teasing with moves that were pleasing. 'OOOOOhhhhhh,' oooohhed the BIG lad.

The lawyer gave him the note and stood back. Nowt happened. 'Read the fucker or I'll chin ya,' opened STIG, reasonably. The lawyer read it, STIG chinned him unconscious and split.

'FUCKIN' BASTARDS-S-S-S-S-S-S-S-S-S,' roared STIG.

Two farm hands arrived. Later on their arms and bodies strolled up, clocked the fallen brief and wondered at his grief.

'What did he do to blow STIG's top and get chinned into the slop?' howled one hand.

'He read this,' hammered the other hand, grabbing the note which was afloat, in a puddle of water beside a goat.

'It says....'Dear STIG, we've heard that your sister is dancing on telly tonight. Could you tell us if it's true cos we'd really hate to miss the fun. Love, The Police.'

The farm hands looked at each other. 'FUCKIN' BASTARDS-S-S-S-S-S-S,' they roared.

Later, STIG BIG burst into his home, throwing the door back and splattering his mother FLO BIG against three feet of wall, four feet of sofa and five feet of the family portrait, which only measured four inches by five inches. FLO whimpered and wailed in the corner just like a Mum in a film when she's brought up her lad only to see him spring into manly action, put his neck on the line, stick his mighty jaw out and grunt a lot.

'No BIG lad, no,' she wailed, STIG stuck out his mighty jaw and grunted. Then he sprang into action up the stairs, ripped open a drawer and sorted in his father's clothes. EDDIE BIG had been a big man, it had taken five police to hold him down and six to kill him. Even then Steady EDDIE had been unlucky. The sixth copper had stuck in his throat. Now his son STIG, his blood boiling to boiling point was ratching in his Dad's gear.

'Yeah,' grunted STIG, finding them. Dropping his trousers where he stood and baring his mighty scrotum to the street STIG BIG slipped into his father's solid canvas y-fronts, pushed his wailing mother aside and set out for vengeance,

IN THE UNDERPANTS OF A DEAD MAN!!!!

Later, STIG BIG, burst into the police station splattering a copper over three feet of wall, four feet of floor and ten feet that were running to try and repel STIG. 'No, BIG lad, no,' wailed the wall of coppers but it was too late. Boiling, belligerent, deranged, maniacal and raving STIG roared down the corridor like a warthog with turpentine on it's bollocks, collecting coppers in a pile and punting the remains into the ceiling where they dripped on the cowering crowd below.
Running for weapons the remaining rozzers re-grouped at the end of the corridor, drew truncheons and shuffled forward to meet the man mountain of destruction that was seething his way towards them. They met him, and wished they hadn't. One copper found his truncheon in his mouth, that was bad enough but he lived just long

enough to regret the fact that STIG had shoved the thing up by way of his arse. Two weaker specimens fainted at the sight and STIG swung their limp forms in a mighty arc fielding flailing truncheons and letting their lifeless limbs whap the other coppers in the balls. Grabbing groins, the pathetic police attack turned it's back and ran. Gathering all their courage they split for the squad cars, drove like fuck for safety and filled their trousers.

'Oi STIG,' mumbled a voice from a locked room.

'Oi TYRONE,' mumbled STIG coming back to something approaching thinking.

'Let us out STIG, we've got stuff to sort.' STIG booted the door to matchwood, sat on the floor and wailed.

'Them bastards got one over on me, they sent me a note asking if my sister was dancing on telly tonight...........the FUCKIN' BAS-TARD-S-S-S-S-S-S-S-S-S-S.'

Meanwhile in the pub the landlord was pushing foaming ale into the faces of the farmhands. 'You should've seen STIG' said one.... 'Mad as fuck, looking for a ruck, gonna kill the coppers and leave them looking yuk!'

'Fucking pathetic,' said the barman, speaking for an entire nation. 'Shut your trap, cut the crap, and let some other joker finish the rap.'

Some other joker did. But, before he started, the posh stranger type that lurks in ropey pubs, asks for 'a pint of beer my Good Man,' and wears jackets that leave you wondering where the fuck they still sell them looking like that, piped up.

'So who exactly is this STIG BIG chappie,' said the posh stranger.

'He's the BIG lad, he's hard as fuck and he's just gone mental vith a vengeance,' frolicked a farm hand. 'The police baited him by the ɔoks of the note lying up at the farm and by my reckoning he'll have educed the local cop shop to shark bait by now.'

'Why would he do that, exactly?' asked the stranger.

'He wouldn't do it exactly,' frigged the farm hand, 'he'd do it ɪore in a rough fashion, by stuffing heads into walls, grabbing and reaking balls, ramming truncheons up rear ends and twisting limbs ɪto impossible bends.'

'No,' said the stranger, 'I mean what would motivate a man to reate a scene like that?'

'The note from the coppers asked if STIG's sister was dancing n telly tonight,' freckled the farmhand.

'FUCKIN' BASTARDS-S-S-S-S-S-S-S-S-S-S-S,' roared the pub.

'So why would STIG's sister be on television?' asked the tranger. Who clearly was a stranger, and looked oddly like the kind of loke who pops up in pubs and that at important moments in films to sk the kind of stupid questions that lead to everybody explaining the ɪissing bits of the story that the people watching the film need to now if the end is gonna make any sense.

The pub looked hard at the stranger.

'My, you country types are a hard looking bunch,' he trembled, etting himself where he stood.

'How can a five foot family portrait measure four inches by five ɪches?' asked the barman.

'Well, em...........,' struggled the stranger.

'Because there are five feet in the portrait. Two on STIG and his ʌum and one foot on his sister, if she's dancin' on telly tonight it'll be ɪe pogo or nowt, and if STIG heard talk like this in his local we'd all e flailing on the floor shouting 'Where in shitting crikey are my legs?'

'Yeah,' added a farmhand, packing years of story into less than a minute. 'The talk is that one night when STIG and his TWIN sister, STELLA BIG, were babies, their Mum and Dad went out, got good and drunk, beat on one too many coppers and ended up sleeping it off in a cell. They got bailed the following morning, got out, went home and looked in on the babies that hadn't been fed. STIG always did have an appetite on him but by the time the BIG's got home STIG hadn't much appetite left and STELLA hadn't much of her right leg left.'

'It was the right,' roared the pub.

'I said that,' fugged the farmhand.

'You said left,' roared the pub.

'I said she didn't have much of her right leg left,' he repeated.

'You said left again,' roared the pub.

'Shut up it was a shit joke the first time,' grunted the farmhand honestly. Then he narrowed his eyes, put on a deep serious voice with just the right amount of local accent and looked behind him like he was nervous. If he had been in a film the camera would have gone in close cos this would have been the bit when he let some deep dark secret about another person slip.

'It's said,' said the farmhand, 'that since that time, STIG's had the taste for human meat. Anyway, that's what's said.'

'I know,' stabbed the stranger, 'You've just said it.'

'It was the right leg,' roared the pub.

'Aw FUCK OFF........................'

40 - SEX

SHARON GOER was ready to go. VINCE EAGER was feeling eager. He pointed at himself and pointed between SHARON's legs. She looked at him. He pointed at himself and pointed between her legs.

'I get it, you're an eager beaver,' she gushed.

'And a half,' he pushed. 'Get your gob round me throb and give some slop to me purple top,' he pulsated majestically. 'Lap up me crotch conkers until I'm nearly bonkers and let your top fall open so I can get a feel of yer stonkers.'

'Nah,' she nibbled hardly noodling, 'let's just go for a good hard fuck.'

They did. Her damp chest heaved in her flimsy top and her mouth was hungry for his as his fingers fumbled into the moist depths between her legs. Her skirt and underwear hit the floor silently as the juices ran down the inside of her legs and he pushed himself inside her with ease and eagerness. He felt the heated excitement deep within her and the tension building to bursting point. She felt the firmth and power inside herself and opened wide to savour every inch of contact. Her nails dug into his shoulders and her loins forced themselves hard against his pelvis as pulsating waves of orgasmic power shook her body from the inside. She threw her head back and moaned out loud as the waves of delight broke against the inside of her skin.

He stayed silent, strong and still inside her.

'You know what we were talking about before,' she mumbled into his ear, 'I think the word is gravitas.'

'Huh?,' he grunted in confusion, 'Nah, that's not it.'

His need was more urgent now but she still lingered in the fading waves of her massive orgasm and the strength of his strokes shook her at first.

'Slowly,' she mumbled. He tried it slowly, his blood raced and the feel of her nipples pushing hard into his chest was driving him wil The firmness of her breasts set the nerves in his torso into a cold tingling frenzy as he pushed deeper inside her and felt her heavy breat on his neck. The dampness inside her left him sliding unstoppably and their rhythm built to a frenzy, but she was ready for it by now and her loud moans came in time with his mighty thrusts, louder and louder a the knot of tension in her firm body built to bursting and then exploded with a force that left her out of control. She screamed, writhed and oozed in ecstatic confusion as VINCE held her tightly an treasured every damp instant of contact inside her and the gripping union of their thrashing bodies.

Throwing her head back onto the soaking pillow, she sighed hard and looked up at him, solid and majestic above her.

'Grimalkin, was it grimalkin?'

'Nah,' he parried, 'That's not it.'

This time he felt the force move within him. Her searing orgasms had left her limp and willing and the growing softness in her touch brought new depths to his pleasure. She stroked his spine with delicate tingling touches that kept his senses alive. Moving slowly beneath him now, she cared only for his pleasure and offered herself totally, spreading her legs wide, opening her arms, pushing her breasts into him and softly kissing his neck. The warmth inside her excited hi beyond mere words and he felt himself pushing to his limits as she gasped at his penetration. The wave of pleasure was upon him now ar e twisted as he filled her. She hung on, feeling his pleasure and loving ıe strength of the wave that broke over her insides and told her she ˙as the most beautiful woman he had ever held in this way.

'Uh,' she flopped back in complete satisfaction. 'Gratuitous, ıat's it, gratuitous.'

'What,' he whispered.

'Gratuitous, it's that word I was trying to think of earlier. That ˙ord that means something that's just thrown in when there's no need ɔr it. You know, what we were talking about, like when you see some ɔuple having sex for ages in a film and it doesn't move the story for-˙ard or anything. Gratuitous, that's the word.'

'Yeah,' agreed VINCE, still stunned at the forceful flood that ιad ejected itself from his body.

'S'funny said SHARON, 'you get loads of gratuitous sex in ιovies but you don't see enough of it in books.

41 - FOOD

STIG BIG, ELVIS TWAT and TYRONE HOODLUM were
starving - and a half. They could have eaten a calf. But they didn't.
Instead they headed for the Police canteen and considered their lot.
Having considered their lot for a lot of time they figured they were in
lot of shit. Which was well tight 'cos it was only that morning that
ELVIS TWAT and TYRONE HOODLUM had woken up in heaps of
shit in their cell.

'We're in shit,' grunted ELVIS. 'The Plods have got us fingered
for doing for the other lot and there's people ready to blabber to put u
in the slammer.' It was true. But it was also true that they were starvin
and that the people serving in the police canteen had just done a
collective Linford for the lift. The food sizzled in front of them like a
pile of food sizzling in front of some starving blokes. They grabbed it,
like starving blokes grabbing food.

Forcing his fearsome elbows into the table, STIG stug his way
into a plate of pizza slices. The crispy cheese top shattered in his
massive jaws letting hot mozzarella cheese assault his dulled senses an
bringing his brain back into gear. The rage that had hung before him a
he shattered the cop shop door thinking only of his sister moved away
long enough to allow STIG to appreciate that hot salty taste of an
olive. Smeared in oil and melted cheese the little black salty pearl
bobbed along his tongue, flicking through tastebuds like the ball on a
pinball machine. STIG pictured it in his mind as it moved in his mouth

e bit into the olive and felt a wave of taste flow across his mouth to eet the lingering cheesy waves that were already breaking from the ont and the back. His brain struggled to process so much taste and nt messages off in the wrong direction - not that there were that any directions in STIG's brain to start with.

He thought of the pizza's past and pictured the olive like a pin-ll again.

'Remember that kid playin' pinball who was deaf and that?' he ked the other two, 'What was his name?'

The other RAIDERS OF THE LOW FOREHEAD struggled en TYRONE tutted 'Tommy, that was his name, Tommy. We saw him at time we went down to the seaside and went in the amusements.'

'Yeah,' eased ELVIS, 'That deaf dumb and blind kid sure plays a ean pinball.'

'But nicking his winnings is a piece of piss,' slobbered STIG ith a mighty laugh.

It was true. The mighty feast in the police canteen was giving ck strength and making them keen for more action. Remembering aside trips, wasps in their beer and other peoples noses ripped off and uck into their pockets was restoring the wholesome, friendly side to e trio. 'When we fight, we fuckin fight, right?' Grunted ELVIS.

Later, full of food and in a better mood, they thought things rough. The Plods had something on them, bodies, a bent bus and itnesses. It was serious but they weren't gonna quit over that. YRONE surveyed a pile of paper on a table and recognized the house. here's some dead gnomes live at that house,' tittered TYRONE, 'I ould know, I killed 'em. There's a bloke with no nose lives there too.'

'How does he smell?' spouted STIG.

'Terrible,' teased TYRONE. How they laughed at TYRONE's riginal and inventive little joke.

They stared at the papers, then they looked at them. They thought about the information in them. Really they thought that if one of them could read and write properly they might find some information in them. This could be important because the picture of the house was next to some pictures of crushed gnomes and TYRONE could just about make out his own name but a lot of the other words were too hard for him.

There was a shuffling sound in the doorway and the trio caught sight of a copper. Like lightning they were on him, over him and threw him. It was STIG BIG who threw him. The airborne Plod flailed and farted thinking he would join the dear departed. 'Let's kill him and then figure out if we wanna torture him later,' grunted ELVIS intelligently.

'It'll be one less to strim yer stepdad's lawn the next time he can't be arsed himself,' reasoned TYRONE. 'Anyway, I'll bet this one can read.'

He could and he offered to read owt that would get him out alive. Filling his police trousers to bursting, the Plod uttered and muttered his way to safety.

'This is a report and it says the lot of you are hard as fuck, TYRONE trashes garden gnomes and noses and there are people willing to spill the beans on you,' pushed the Plod.

'If they spill the beans on me I'll take the open can and shove it up......' STIG didn't get time to finish before the Plod made a break through the window and almost fell out.

'Just when I was gettin' interested,' talked TYRONE taking him by the scruff of the neck and scruffing him up a treat with his feet. Stamped, stumped and getting the hump, the Plod's position in any negotiations was looking limited.

'I'll cop a plea to come out alive, if you'll spare me I won't give you no jive,' he wailed. And he did. In five minutes flat he'd grassed up his mates and told the RAIDERS that the cops were out to get statements from the pummelled pensioners to add to the bits they got from the burger-van man and the shits they'd got looking at the last pile of Plods who'd tangled with the vicious sods that were STIG, ELVIS d TYRONE.

The copper spilled the lot in five minutes flat. Five minutes later
 was flat on his back, beaten unconscious but still alive and likely to
 his family with a story to tell that would stir the heart of any
 glishman and convince them that tangling with sub-human sorts was
 well dodgy sport.

STIG, ELVIS and TYRONE had simply given the plod a playful
 ing over to warm up for the main event - they had their tender and
 oughtful side like that.

42 - VIOLENCE

SHARON GOER, LITTLE JOHNNY GOER, MR GOER and VINCE EAGER were having a summit meeting.

'Why are we having a summit meeting?' grunted Mr GOER.

'Cos there's summit we want to tell you,' slopped SHARON pathetically.

She told her Dad about ELVIS' mighty shit slopping and the way he walked out of the Bulimic Bengali, later she threw in descriptions of the strength and total lack of morals of the RAIDERS OF THE LOW FOREHEAD and talked about the way that VINCE had made her come so much she thought the walls were moving.

MR GOER talked crispy Woodpeckers and LITTLE JOHNNY gushed FRENCH FRANK and fancied a wank. Since they were all taking together nobody heard anything. LITTLE JOHNNY thought the whole thing reminded him about the pointlessness of all human life - ever. He thought about making some huge work of art with lots of people walking around talking and not doing anything with their lives. He reckoned he'd get rich and famous for coming up with this idea and everyone would understand and life would change for the better, allowing a man to stand next to his fellow man, put his tongue down his throat and not damage his chances of being a highly respected bus driver. Then he looked out at a prison landing and realised he was a few centuries too late with the idea and nobody gave a shit anyway. But apart from that, the squalor of prison and the total injustice of him being there in the first place life was just one top grin.

'Shut up and listen,' screamed SHARON. They all shut up, listened and realised that nobody saying anything was about as fucking pointless as everybody saying something. They were getting nowhere in terms of springing LITTLE JOHNNY and MR GOER but they were definitely learning something about the deeper side of life. Except they were too shallow to figure it out.

'JOHNNY's turned, permanent,' grunted Mr GOER. 'He's met this bloke called FRENCH FRANK and that's about the size of it.' VINCE and SHARON looked at the gap between Mr GOER's hands and almost fainted.

'Are you gonna spring us or what, VINCE,' grunted Mr GOER. Let's face it, if this was a TV movie you'd be planning your final move and getting ready to splat the twats that upon us have shat.'

'Yeah,' grunted VINCE, 'and your one liners wouldn't be so heinous.'

'For fuck's sake VINCE,' screamed Mr GOER, 'are you a man or a mouse?'

'Dunno,' grunted VINCE, 'Pass me the cheese and I'll think about it.'

'Look,' said JOHNNY, 'If you're gonna beat those gits who put us here you'll have to spring into action and feel no fear. You'll have to leap into a scrum without tasting fright and not stop swinging till you see the seventh shade of shite.'

Grabbing VINCE by the hair LITTLE JOHNNY dragged him down to the gym where blokes were being blokes. These were hard men, toughened by years of prison. Men who knew no shame, felt no remorse and cleaned their teeth most nights with solid manly strokes.

'These blokes can teach you about being hard,' jibbed JOHNNY. And he was right.

'What's that ponce doing in here?' roared the gym. The hardened criminals set about teaching VINCE. ''Ere son,' punch this sports bag and harden up your hands,' carped a convict. VINCE let fly, and started to cry as the heavy duty nylon made his hands fry.

'He's softer than the ring-stinging result of a dozen bars of laxative chocolate,' punched a prisoner, honestly.

And he was.

VINCE gave it all he had. He ripped into the wall bars with passion and thoughts of a life time of glorious gobbling from SHARON's gums. He pulled, tugged, heaved and hrmmphed his way up the bars with all the aggro he could gather, then gave up on the third level. Later, he tried to beat the shit out of a punch bag and moved at least three grains of dust but definitely no more than seven. Then he exploded onto the judo mat to face down an aging armed robber with a dodgy hip and a boil on his lip. The robber won on a technical knockout when VINCE almost shat himself at the thought of the fight spoiling his haircut.

Facing up to his reflection in the mirror of the gents, VINCE breathed hard, let out a blood curdling scream, ripped open the cold tap and threw water on his face fast and hard.

'I'm a man, I'm a man and I must do what I can,' he roared in defiance of the overwhelming odds facing him. He screamed out to the judo mat, clocked the aging hard man waiting to face him down, flew at the fossil with a two-handed blast of furious fistful action and fell flat on his face when the old git sank him with the slowest head-butt in history.

Clocking the action a muttering axe murderer moved in.
'If you're gonna face down ELVIS, TYRONE and STIG,' he muttered. 'I think I can help out.'

'How's that?' said VINCE with a wince.

'Easy, Son,' he said slipping him a piece of paper. 'This is the address of my bail hostel. I'm out in another week. Give this to LITTLE JOHNNY's sister. Once them three nutters have torn you limb from limb she'll be a bit lonely and I'll give her a right good seeing to any-time she's up for it.'

43 - SEX

VINCE skulked out of the prison lower than a legless dog. A legless dog being pulled along by its owner clocked VINCE and commented 'Life's a drag, eh?'

It could have been worse, VINCE didn't understand dog. He felt the shame of failure upon him and the watery slops of total fear straining at his ring-piece. He also felt SHARON's matchlessly firm body rub up against him in a narrow alleyway. They walked home in silence, shagged up to point seven on the Richter scale and rated it a failure by their high standards.

'Dunno what it is,' violated VINCE, 'but the thought of those bastards heartlessly ripping me apart and enjoying every second of the senseless cruelty seems to stop my love pump lasting more than fifteen minutes at full length.'

Later, VINCE found himself in a cinema, in a state of trouble, complicated by agitation, botheration, degradation and cheap after-shave. He picked at his tasteless popcorn and panted at the massive jugs on the cinema screen. They belonged to some woman on a train and the firm ripples shaking her nipples were timed to perfection with the train's insurrection - well the sound of it's wheels really. The picture cut to a young lad getting up from opposite the girl, dropping his pants in the train's toilet and.....OH FUCK!!!!!!!! VINCE's blood ran cold as he realised that the lad was him and remembered that tug on a train when his jeans couldn't take the strain of the massive throbbing thrust he'd got looking at that bust. The audience laughed in a ripple and VINCE clocked some nipples, the same ones that were on the screen and they were looming in front of him as he sat there in his cinema seat. He felt the shame and wanted to scream.

The girl from the train was standing in front of him, looking the same but smiling from ear to ear. The picture on the screen changed, now VINCE was in the bath, a mag was on the floor opened to the middle pages. He reached into the foam, the water started to splash about, he threw back his head and the whole cinema laughed out loud.........except VINCE. Two seats in front a naked girl turned round and waved, it was her from the centre-fold. Dimly VINCE looked around. Every seat in the cinema was filled with lasses, fit ones at that, he recognized every one of them as girls he'd rated and thought about when he fancied a five fingered........OOH FUCKIN' HELL!!!!!!!!!! This film of every sordid wank in his fairly average life was gonna last days. No man could take that much shame, the shame he felt in that seat, taking the heat. He sprang up, or at least he tried. He noticed he was strapped in. The lasses were loving every moment and he'd just spotted SHARON two rows away, right next to CINDY CRAWFORD. He tried to make sense of the whole sorry mess and figured they'd already killed him and he'd gone to Hell. It had to be. Near his feet on the floor DEBBIE DOWNES, slag of the town, was crawling and falling and rolling around.

'Oi VINCE' she drooled, remember that time I gave you a flash of my knickers and then I caught you later with your hands in your coat at the bus shelter?'

He did, it was coming up on the screen and the crowd was chanting, 'Wanker, WANKer, WANKER!!, WANKER!!!!!!!!'

'Wanker, wanker,' mumbled VINCE as SHARON shook him awake.

'VINCE,' screamed SHARON, 'I've just seen ELVIS, TYRONE and STIG raiding their low foreheaded way towards the hall at the top of the road. If you get out there and sort them out I'll gobble your load, for good.'

VINCE clocked the flat, the armchair where he'd fallen asleep and SHARON's gravity defying cleavage.

'Wanker,' he mumbled still half-dreaming. 'I'm a wanker.'

'You could be,' she shimmied, 'but you've got a chance to make something of yourself, be someone, be remembered. Oh VINCE, peopl say you're no good, they say you're a scrawny loser who'd pay a pensioner to fake a dive in a chip shop in a pathetic attempt to prove yourself hard. People say you've got a body from a famine relief poster and what little brains you have are in your bollocks, people say you once got so drunk at a party that you took a dump on the floor and go thrown out for trying to eat it like a banana. But listen VINCE, between my legs there's a million nerve ends that know different. There's a few gallons of moisture that flood for you every day, there's a permanent dampness in that place that most blokes don't even know exists and there's several pairs of crusty panties waiting to be washed. All of them in their own way are crying out to the world 'VINCE EAGER has what it takes to be a real man.' There may be three psychopathic thugs out there who swat hardened police like flies off shi but VINCE, I believe in you. If you can do to that trio what you do to my senses every time you stroke my inner thighs I think we have a chance.

She fell exhausted at his feet, face down with her legs together. Summoning deep reserves of heroism VINCE surveyed her curvy but collapsed carcass. Almost growling like a man he spoke.

'I'll never manage a jump with her in that position. Suppose I'c better head outside and get myself torn limb from limb in a totally pointless attempt at stopping the three hardest bastards that ever claimed they were three hard bastards from doing more hard bastard stuff.'

44 - FOOD

On his way out of the door VINCE grabbed a ginger nut biscuit off the table. Normally, he would have savoured the flavour but knowledge of the nutters just outside the shutters, was doing in his brains and making him stutter.

'G-g-g-ginger nut,' he stam-am-am-amered. It snapped in his teeth and sent a pain right round his gob. He winced at the agony, remembered he really was as soft as shite and wondered where exactly you applied for them jobs at the South Pole that went on for months and let everybody forget that you'd ever lived.

In a desperate attempt to be a hero he headed for the fridge and ripped out a beer - a ginger beer. He blocked it in one, belched and roared heroically. 'THERE'S NOWT TASTES LIKE GINGER BEER!!!!!' he screamed. He was wrong - of course - but then he'd never tasted diabetic piss and Slimline Tonic with ice.

45 - VIOLENCE

At the top of the street, in a hall, the pensioners had a meeting, for a ball. The hospital had turfed them out after they were caught selling tickets to their mates and sneaking them in for hot baths, hot food and hot sex action. It was the last of these that had given the scam away when one of the doddery old biddies asked for an extra pint of custard because she'd run out of KY jelly.

That self same biddy was the same one who'd seen ELVIS, TYRONE and STIG coming on the scene of the trashed bus and told as much to the police inspector. He hadn't been so impressed at the time but with little else to go on the inspector was now ready to grab any witness who could help him bang up the RAIDERS OF THE LOW FOREHEAD. The old biddie - SLAGGIE AGGIE to her mates - could be talked into talking.

The pensioners had gathered for a tea dance, they had the tea, a few Vera Lynn CDs and ten pints of stolen hospital custard. Were they gonna score this afternoon or what!!!!! SLAGGIE AGGIE stood at the door, stared into the drizzle and started to sing.
'Raindrops is fallin' on me head,' she grated.

The police inspector was strolling up to the tea dance. SLAGGIE swayed down to meet him, singing all the time.
'It won't be long till A PENIS steps out to greet me,' she grunted stroking his strong trousers somewhere near his police box.

'Is that a truncheon in your pocket or are you just pleased to see......'

'It's a truncheon,' he talked, fast. 'Look, SLAGGIE, I've just heard on the radio that those three thugs have escaped, I've got to get them and put them away before they put this whole town down. You saw them, would you say so in court?'

'What's in it for me?' grunted AGGIE pushing hard for a deal and looking hard for the outline of his bollocks.

'What do you want AGGIE?'

'A good stiff cock between me legs.'

'My brothers a farmer, he's got a chicken with arthritis, I'll see what I can do.'

Her jaw dropped, she would have told him where to stick it but a brick came sailing through the air, parted AGGIE's hair and didn't stop there. It hit the door, skidded on the floor, AGGIE and the cop couldn't believe what they saw. There was a police badge stuck on the brick and a note, it said:

'Psycho 2 Plod 2 - penalty shoot-out.'

An old bloke taking tickets on the door looked up and clocked the commotion. He was reading a paper. A pink coloured paper. From a distance he looked a right toff and people thought he had a well posh head. That was tight really cos all he did was collect old papers, leave them near a window for a year and then read them when he was out. He was full of pathetic poses like that.

AGGIE, the pink paper poser and the inspector looked, and saw, three big figures. The three lookers figured the three figures were big. The three big figures looked at the three lookers. From somewhere inside the hall the sound of Vera Lynn, sweetheart of the forces in World War II, started up.

'We'll meet again,' wailed Vera on the sound system.

'So, we meet again,' spouted STIG, which was a well crap line cos he'd never met this inspector before.

AGGIE, the cop and the pink paper poser gathered all their courage, ran inside, bolted the door and headed for the bogs to drop some logs. A Transit load of police stormed in the back entrance around the same time the RAIDERS OF THE LOW FOREHEAD were smashing the front door into the floor. Caught in the crossfire the pensioners stood still, like a bunch of pensioners caught in some cross-fire.

'We're the RAIDERS OF THE LOW FOREHEAD and you lot are dead!' howled ELVIS, TYRONE and STIG. Everyone in the hall was still alive, but they got the general idea. TYRONE tore across the floor cos he'd seen a cop and wanted to even the score. The cop in question was a blonde bloke who'd once ended TYRONE's best attempt at a master stroke.

When SIR CLEMENT had put TYRONE in charge of the family garage business, TYRONE had come up with a corker of a cack brained, deranged, dis-arranged scam that almost left him maimed. Figuring that low mileage, decent motors conned bigger bucks from the voters, he'd planned a little earner. On his first night in charge of HOODLUM GARAGE SERVICES he'd gathered the mechanics and muttered 'We'll spend the hours of darkness reversing the second hand motors and in the morning the lowered mileages will push up the prices.' The mechanics thought about telling TYRONE that he'd need an extra brain just to qualify as a fuck-wit, thought about their over-time, and kept their gobs shut. A month later, TYRONE sold the garage to pay off seventeen fines for dangerous driving, SIR CLEMENT dropped a brace of high class hookers off at the Chief Constable's country retreat, and the highest of the high class hookers opened her bra to reveal the words 'Don't jail TYRONE' plastered on the enormity of her ample frontage.

'Get the picture?' panted SIR CLEMENT.

'Dunno,' chanted the Chief, 'I'm a bit short sighted, she'd bette stick that message right in my face.'

This matters for two reasons:

i - It's a while since this story had any gratuitous sex.

ii - The copper who'd copped seventeen second hand sets of speeding wheels driving backwards in search of lucrative deals was now facing TYRONE and making him groan.

'You're the big blonde bastard that nicked me and the mechanics, slapped us in cuffs and made us panic,' terrorised TYRONE.

'Just doin' me job, son,' cackled the copper. TYRONE sprang, slashed, scrummed and mashed. Later he ripped, rubbed, butted and battered before tearing the copper and leaving him scattered. He wouldn't be doin' his job anymore.

STIG and ELVIS covered ground, ripped off limbs and threw them around. 'SHEEP SHAGGER AGGRO!!!!!,' screamed STIG, honestly.

A fast and furious fistful fracas rumbled with a rhythm like some shaking moracas. ELVIS TWAT shook some beans, willy beans, that were still attached to a copper. Later the copper shook with fury, hit ELVIS full in the face and broke three of his own fingers.

'Don't hit them in the heads, there's nowt worth damaging in here,' screamed a sergeant. 'Go for the goolies, its your only hope, lads.' They tried, but it was hopeless.

VINCE stood in the doorway. Fists were flying, and so were coppers. VINCE drew himself up to his full height, thought hard about the need for courage, thought of SHARON, his manhood and a lifetime of luscious lippings. If he was ever gonna have a moment, this was it. He gathered every ounce of courage, breathed deeply and ran like fuck in the other direction.

Vera Lynn played as TYRONE, ELVIS and STIG swayed, slashed, booted, blasted, broke, bashed, splintered and slashed some more on their way through the constabulary's finest. Facing down a king sized plod with an attitude to match, TYRONE tore trousers, ripped flesh, broke an arm and screamed 'BANGLADESH,' he had no idea what it meant. Later he pummelled, rumbled, rolled and tumbled into the copper. After that he got bored and killed him.

Outside a UFO full of green-eyed squid aliens skidded to a halt
'There's the sound of Vera, the sight of a fight, this combination suggests we were right,' spluttered a slobbering squid.
A gaggle of green tentacled monsters slithered inside and clocked the carnage.
'Take us to Vera,' demanded the leader, pushing a particle beam weapon into the face of a plod. The plod in question was the inspector on his way out of the bogs. He gawped at the greenies, sighted their saucer and screamed 'Oi!'.
Those plods with eyes still in their sockets swivelled and sighted the same thing. All of these plods had seen a note from their boss stating that the best witness to the RAIDERS recent atrocities had also claimed a squid-related UFO sighting and was - therefore - a dodgy bet in court. Now, with the evidence slithered up to the door and was waving it's tentacles so the police knew they could be onto something.

'Vera Lynn, Vera Lynn,' chanted the squid types. Suspending all movement with a deft blast from a dodgy weapon, the commander cut a cool waddle through the halted action, ripped a CD case from the stack and brought it back. The green eyed throng read the titles of the songs, then they turned over the case, and screamed at the creases in the face of the woman who had brought them to this place.

'She's older than this lot and she's lost what she's got,' screamed a squid, pointing at the pensioners.

'She's lost what she had,' corrected the commander. 'She had it, and it's gone. That's relativity, and it stinks like fuck.'
Disappointed, depressed and not wearing a vest, the commander had figured out one serious scientific principle. He waved his weapon and re-started the fight, leading his troops out across the galaxy again.

'Now we've cracked relativity, Boss, we should deal with nother of the big questions,' squirted a squid. 'Like what happens vhen an unstoppable force meets an immovable object.'

'Good idea,' agreed the commander, 'but I think we'll give this lanet a wide one in future, we'll learn nothing from these morons.'

Stunned for a second, the fighters fought to a standstill. They ould have sworn they'd seen some green-eyed squid. Only now the oorway was empty. Those with brains stopped and thought. Those vithout didn't. Which gave an advantage to TYRONE, ELVIS and STIG. Headbutting hard TYRONE whapped a WPC below the knee. Dimly he remembered something his Dad had said.
'Women,' SIR CLEMENT spat, 'can't live with 'em, can't ury 'em under the floorboards.'

It made sense at the time but it was confusing the fuck out of TYRONE now cos' he'd only butted the police lass once and she was lready half way through the floor boards. Given this floorboard enetration with one head butt, burying her would be a piece of piss.

The coppers re-grouped, built barricades and mounted guerilla ttacks, the fight slowed down and moved to an exchange of missiles. The unstoppable force of the RAIDERS met an immovable object. The orce forced, the object resisted. TYRONE, ELVIS and STIG stopped utting and biting and did some uniting. 'We'll take 'em together, down he middle of the barricade,' ELVIS sayed. The trio tore down the hall, ounced off a wall, butted the barricade and made it all fall. Without rotection the Police pissed themselves, gagged on the smell, turned heir backs and ran like hell. The RAIDERS ran outside after the ounding Bill. 'We're on 'em,' screamed ELVIS, getting on 'em. Death vas gonna come to the local constabulary on a colossal scale. ut..........

VINCE was coming up the street, he was driving a tractor he'd icked from the farm and under his arm, was STIG's sheep.

'MY PRETTY DARLIN,' screamed STIG.

'You bastards make another move and the sheep gets it,' volumed VINCE.

'Fuck the sheep,' talked TYRONE, slugging a sergeant.

'What if I do,' wailed STIG, toppling TYRONE with a thump and groan.

'What's got into you BIG lad?' eased ELVIS, confused and ...confused.

WHUMP!!!!!!!!!!

ELVIS was laid low with a mighty blow. Slobbering, blubbering and in need of some mothering STIG jumped on ELVIS and started to smother him.

'Confess, STIG,' vectored VINCE. 'Tell these coppers that you framed Mr GOER and LITTLE JOHNNY for a crime they didn't commit, pummelled a load of pensioners and dumped them in the shit, confess you offed the plods in quite impressive style and that the RAIDERS OF THE LOW FOREHEAD have reeked terror all the while. Confess or sheep get's it.'

'I confess,' screamed STIG pulling polaroids from pockets and throwing evidence in the face of the disbelieving cops.
'The GOER two did nowt, us three pulled the robbery and threatened the witnesses so we could stay free. ELVIS fought for breath, VINCE remembered his session suffocating under his Aunty Dorothy and briefly felt sympathy for ELVIS.

Later, with a statement printed off at the police station, STIG was allowed to stroke a foot of fleece. When they'd revived ELVIS and TYRONE, showed them STIG's statement and watched them rattle their handcuffs, vent their spleen, see they were trapped and start looking mean, they let the BIG LAD have her in the cell for ten minutes. It wasn't much reward for grassing his mates, ending a remorseless reign of terror and restoring peace to a town that had never had it in the first place so it couldn't really be restored. Then again, it was ten minutes and she was a serious looking piece of fleece.

Soon after that MR GOER and LITTLE JOHNNY GOER got the word. And the word was with a Vicar in Kickers.

'I'm a right soft touch and I'm daft enough to visit the criminally insane and then go on telly telling the world why these nutters should be released cos really they're okay,' opened the Vicar when he got to the jail.

'Don't open in here....,' started MR GOER.

'Fuck off, I've heard it,' closed the Vic.

When the Vic told 'em they were free to go, MR GOER went mad and LITTLE JOHNNY went all sad. Feeling up FRENCH FRANK - The man from Paris with the tasty piece of Aris - LITTLE JOHNNY gazed in his eyes and glugged his goodbyes.

Even later still, the cops considered their position. They were together in a room. The RAIDERS were apart, chained down in separate cells. Two totally chained and STIG bound to a bench with a turnip on his tool, his darlin' by his side and a smile on his face. He was getting his action in return for a non-stop commentary on RAIDERS action over the years. Some cops were considering SIR CLEMENT HOODLUM's return in two weeks. They figured they'd better work fast to crack ELVIS and TYRONE.

'Stick lumps of metal in their mouths and live wires up their arses,' suggested one cop.

'Smear their knobs with honey and send in the soldier ants,' spluttered a second.

'Rub 'em over with a cheese grater and spray them with Domestos,' thudded a third.

After half an hour the cops had made one decision. 'Get in a pile of cans and some serious curries, we're gonna have a fun fortnight,' chuckled the chief.

Even later still, VINCE, SHARON, MR GOER and LITTLE JOHNNY met for crisps and beer and the rump of a steer. 'This is some steak,' munched MR GOER.

'Yeah,' dribbled SHARON, and this is some man, she stroked VINCE. 'In true heroic fashion he's triumphed over incredible odds, brought disaster to some evil sods, used his wits and used his might, ooh I hope he'll pump me full tonight.'

And they all lived happily for the next 23 minutes.

ATTACK!

This generation needs a NEW literature - writing that apes, matches, parodies and supersedes the flickeringly fast 900 MPH ATTACK! ATTACK ATTACK! velocity of early 21st century popular culture at its most mEnTaL!

HARD-CORE ANARCHO-COMMIE SEX PULP!

We will publish writers who think they're rock stars, rock stars who think they're writers and we will make supernovas of the stuttering, wild-eyed, slack-jawed drooling idiot-geek geniuses who lurk in the fanzine/internet shadows.

HORROR! SEX! WAR! DRUGS! VIOLENCE!

"Subtlety" is found in the dictionary between "shit" and "syphilis".

VICTORY OR DEATH!

The self-perpetuating ponce-mafia oligarchy of effete bourgeois wankers who run the 'literary scene' must be swept aside by a tidal wave of screaming urchin tits-out teenage terror totty and DESTROYED!

ATTACK! ATTACK! ATTACK!

COMING FROM
ATTACK!
IN 2000 AD!